Blessings from the Wrong Side of Town

C.S. KJAR

Editor: JoEllen Claypool
Cover Designed by jimmygibbs
Proofreading by John Buchanan

Available in eBook and Paperback

ISBN-13: 978-1532824845
ISBN-10: 153282484X

http://www.cskjar.com

Dedicated to everyone who has lived at least five decades. May future decades bring you laughter, fun, and good health.

Alfred Henry Watson

Alfred "Al" Henry Watson died Saturday, June 6, at his home surrounded by his children. He was born on September 18, 1932 in Fairview, Texas and spent the rest of his life there except for a stint in the U.S. Army.

Al dropped out of school in the eighth grade to help his father on the farm. When he turned 18, he was drafted into the Army. He was a veteran of the Korean Conflict and received a Purple Heart for injuries suffered there. After he returned from the war, he worked as an apprentice, learning the trade of electrician.

Al married Shirley Benton in 1953 and they had four children. He worked at Smith Electric for 40 years before retiring. He and Shirley enjoyed traveling and visiting their grandchildren.

Al was preceded in death by his parents and one son, Neal, who was killed in Viet Nam. His survivors include his wife, Shirley, his children Sam, Sadie, and Kay and their spouses. He had 10 grandchildren and two great-grandchildren.

Funeral services will be held on Tuesday, June 5, at 10:00 a.m. in the Creekside Baptist Church, followed by burial at the Hilltop Cemetery. The Christian Church Group will provide a luncheon after the burial. In lieu of flowers, the family requests donations be made to the VFW of Fairview.

1

"I wonder what it feels like to die."

Betty Drummond nonchalantly tossed the question out into the minivan as her younger sister, Leona Templeton, drove along the streets of Fairview. Betty's pale hair looked whiter against her black dress. She stared out the window at the passing brick houses with their manicured lawns. She stroked her chin while the sunlight flickered on and off her face as the minivan passed under the shade trees.

Breaking out of her daydream, Betty looked at Leona and asked, "I wonder if the soul floats away or if it goes kicking and screaming?"

Leona put on the blinker and turned a corner. Dressed in her black funeral dress, she pushed a stray strand of her white hair back into place while thinking of an answer in response. "I've read that it's peaceful and that you should go toward the light." She glanced in the rearview mirror at Clarence Brown in his usual place, in the backseat behind Betty. The old gentleman in his dark blue suit and plaid tie had a thoughtful look on his face.

Clarence cleared his throat like he always did before he spoke authoritatively. "It depends on where you're going," he said. "If you're going to heaven, I think the angels come for you and you're happy to fly toward the light with them. If demons show up, you'll probably be clawing and hanging on to stay. You probably already feel the heat of the hell fires." He nodded like he'd just given the answer to the question of life. "Yes, sir, that's what I think."

Betty gasped, turning as far as she could in the seat to look back at him. Her 77-year-old neck wouldn't turn that far, so she looked at him out of the side of her eye. "Why Clarence, you're so wise! I've never thought of it that way." She turned around and leaned back in her seat, sighing, "I hope angels come for me someday."

"They will, Betty," Clarence said. "You're a good woman." He looked out the window and mindlessly tapped his fingers on the armrest. "I hope to see them too."

Leona glanced in the rearview mirror again. She really wasn't in the mood to discuss the topic. No one knew what it was like to die so how could anyone talk about it intelligently. The morbid topic left her feeling full of ugly butterflies. It made her heart ache.

"I read the obituaries most every day," Betty said in a musing voice, "I see more and more people that I know in there. I remember the days when only old people died. Now it's people our age. That's so sad." Betty looked at her sister as she stopped for a red light. "Doesn't it seem that way to you, Leona?"

Leona rolled her eyes and hoped her sister hadn't seen it.

"I've notice that too," Clarence declared from the back. "Mostly young people die nowadays. Regrettable. I wonder what changed to make it so?"

Leona stopped for a red light and glanced at the 79-year-old man in the rearview mirror again, wondering what age he considered to be old. She sighed, wondering if she could redirect the conversation. It wouldn't be an easy task. They were on their way home from Al's funeral, a man they'd known since grade school when he and their older brother became best friends. The age of watching your friends pass and wondering when your time will come. The age of losing a spouse.

Death had already taken her husband Joe away. Their 56 years of marriage had passed so quickly. They married right out of high school so she had never known adult life without him. Now she was left alone with her widowed sister and the widower who lived across the street, chauffeuring them around town and listening to their strange conversations about death.

Leona felt desperately in need of a shower. Ever since her Joe died two years ago, her distaste for funerals had turned to abhorrence. Each one meant someone was feeling the same heartache she was. She always rushed home after funerals to shower away the smells and the tears, the hugs and the handshakes, the feelings and the heartaches. She needed to wash away the unhappiness and the sense of loss. And the recurring thought to instigate her own funeral sooner rather than later.

She'd taken a lot of extra showers in the past two years because the deaths kept coming. People she'd grown up with. People she'd met years ago. People she hardly knew. She had to attend their funerals. It was her duty. It was her church group's duty. A never-ending duty.

She felt a light touch on her arm. "Are you all right?" Betty's voice was pitched high with concern. "I asked you a question. Oh, and now the light's green."

Leona pulled herself out of her dark philosophical pit and drove on. "I thought Al's funeral was very nice. And the flowers on the casket were beautiful." It was her chance to change the topic. "The flowers reminded me that we need to set our flower pots out and get them ready for planting."

"Poor Shirley." Betty sighed, refusing to leave the talk of death. "How will she ever get along without Al?"

"The same way you get along without Vince and I get along without Joe. She'll adjust to living without him, but

3

she'll miss him sorely until she passes." Leona returned her sister's sigh. "That's why the obituaries calls us the surviving spouse. It's not called living spouses. We're survivors. Our lives are completely changed and we have to find a new normal."

Clarence cleared his throat again. "New normal? There's a term that you never heard in the old days. Just what is that?" His voice grew softer. "Huh…new normal. Who comes up with this stuff?" He kept muttering under his breath, but Leona couldn't make out his words.

"Young people talk funny, don't they?" Betty added. "They should learn to speak proper English while they're in school." Betty shook her head and looked out the side window. "I don't understand some of the new shows on TV. It's like they're talking in a foreign language."

Oh my word! Leona thought as she turned another corner. *I changed the subject, but I'm not sure this one is any better. Griping about how things aren't like the old days. I remember listening to Mom and Dad saying the same thing. The saying has probably been around since the beginning of time.*

"It's harder if the wife dies first," Clarence Brown said, taking the conversation back to its origin. "Men can't take care of themselves as good as women can take care of themselves."

Leona fought the urge to slam on the brakes, get out, and run away from the inane conversation. "Don't start that." She made the last turn down the tree-lined street of older, well-kept homes with their neat lawns and well-tended flowerbeds. "If men can't take care of themselves, it's their own fault. You can rewire a house, build a skyscraper, rebuild a car engine, but you can't run a washing machine? Men are lazy!"

"I'm not lazy!" Clarence began. "It's not a man's job…"

"Hush you two!" Betty, ever the peacekeeper, cried out in a tearful voice. "This is not the time! Poor Shirley needs our sympathy and help. She's lost her husband!" She daubed at her eyes with a tissue. "It's not easy losing your husband."

Leona pulled into the garage alongside of her Joe's beloved 1975 Chrysler Newport, their Sunday-go-to-meeting car. Joe always said it had the luxury and room to make him feel important in the world. He loved that car and babied it like one of their children. Leona started it on occasion to make sure the motor still ran. One of these days, she'd have to take it out and put gas in it. She'd sell it someday, but not today. Not yet anyway.

Relieved to be home, Leona gathered her purse and got out. She went to the back of the minivan to get out the food containers they'd taken to the after-funeral dinner. Betty joined her to get Clarence's walker for him. Clarence struggled out of the minivan and held onto it as he limped to the rear. Taking his walker from Betty, he went down the driveway, his walker wheel squeaking with every turn.

"Clarence!" Leona shouted as he went across the street to his house. "Oil that wheel!"

Clarence waved his hand in the air as if he heard, but Leona knew he hadn't. That's why that wheel went unoiled. He couldn't hear the squeak so in his mind, it didn't exist. Everyone else could hear it and knew well ahead of time that Clarence was coming.

Leona shifted her food containers into her left hand as she unlocked the garage door that led into her kitchen. As soon as she opened the door, she sensed that something wasn't quite right. She hesitated before taking a step inside, looking for clues and listening for sounds, anything that would tell her why the hair on the back of her neck was standing up.

She heard Betty's footsteps coming up behind her. "What are you waiting for?" Betty whispered, peering over Leona's shoulder.

Leona stepped slowly into her kitchen. A glance around

sent a bolt of fear through her. She blinked her eyes several times trying to refocus, hoping that she wasn't really seeing what she was seeing. The view didn't change. She let out a cry. "Oh—oh—oh my WORD!"

Betty scurried up beside her and let out her own cry of disbelief.

Broken china, shattered coffee cups, and silverware were strewn all over the floor. The contents of their cabinets and pantry had been ripped open and poured across the debris and the containers flung against the wall where they left their mark on impact. Flour, sugar, and spices covered everything in the kitchen. The refrigerator door stood open. Everything had been emptied except for the vegetable drawer. Ketchup and mustard slowly oozed down the kitchen walls and stained both the floor and countertops. Eggs had been thrown everywhere. Food-covered footprints tracked into the living room.

Leona set her food containers on the syrup-covered countertop. She held her purse close to make sure it wouldn't bump the sticky mess. The two women crept into the living room, tiptoeing to keep from tracking any more of the mess. The living room was in total disarray, like a tornado had blown through it and upended everything. In the middle of the floor, their gallon of milk was overturned and surrounded by a wet puddle. The furniture upholstery was shredded.

The stench of too much bleach filled the air. Leona put her hand over her nose and mouth and pushed Betty back into the most undisturbed corner of the kitchen.

Both ladies stood for a moment trying to regain their composures. Leona held her hand over her heart to keep it steady. "I'll go check the other rooms," she whispered. She scanned the floor looking for a safe step to take.

"No!" Betty held onto her arm. "Someone might still be in here! Let's go see Clarence and call the police from there." She tugged on Leona's arm until she followed her out of the garage. They hurried across the street as fast as their legs could carry them, waving their purses in the air.

Clarence had just opened his front door when the two women yelled out to him. "Our house has been robbed!" Leona cried out. "Everything is in ruins!"

Clarence's mouth fell open. "What? Are you sure?"

Leona stopped at the edge of the ramp that led to his front porch and put her hands on her hips. "Am I sure? Trust me! I didn't leave my house that way! Oh my word! It's awful!" She wiped the tears from her face before she put her arm around Betty and led her to the front door. "We have to call the police."

Clarence stood wide-eyed in his doorway, glancing first at the two distraught women, then to the house across the street, and back again. He patted Leona with one hand while he held onto his walker with the other. Then he changed hands and patted Betty's hand. "Come in and sit down." He motioned them inside, then shuffled over to the sofa, and pushed a pile of newspapers onto the coffee table.

"Clarence, call the police." Leona dried her eyes a little. "They need to find out who did this."

Clarence fumbled with his pocket and found his cell phone. He pulled it out and flipped it open. "Now, let's see," he said as he tried to focus on the small buttons. "That's nine." He pushed a button. "Oops. That's nine…" He pushed again. "One." He pushed another button. "Oops. Why do they make buttons so small when I have such big fingers?"

"Oh never mind!" Leona got her cell phone out of her purse and dialed 911. "Send the police. I've been robbed! Come quick! Where am I? I'm at 6315 South Harwood Circle. Someone has gone through my house and destroyed it." She paused for a moment. "I don't know if they took anything. I couldn't see past the mess they made to know what's there and what's missing. Just come quickly!"

2

"No! You'll track stuff all over the floor!" Leona cried out. She stood just behind Police Officer Don Janus and his young partner, Olivia Torrez, as they started to enter the kitchen. Her words were a reaction of habit more than anything that made sense. Her brain was so overloaded she couldn't think straight.

Officer Torrez turned to look at her. Her dark brown eyes held sympathy and compassion. "I don't think it'll make much difference."

Leona covered her reddened face with her hands. "Of course it won't. I'm sorry." She felt Officer Torrez give her a soft touch pat on the shoulder and heard the crunch of a footstep in her ruined kitchen.

"Lord, give me strength," Leona whispered to herself. More crunching footsteps across her ruined kitchen brought her thoughts to the situation at hand.

"Wow, they really did a number, didn't they?" Officer Janus said to his partner. "Did you put in a call for Detective Smythe?"

"Yes, before we got out of the car," Officer Torrez said. They had their guns ready in case someone was still in the house. She motioned for Leona to go back into the garage.

The officers cautiously crept into the living room, with Leona not far behind them. She held up her pant legs so they wouldn't be stained with ketchup or any other substance. The polyester pants were only a year old and she didn't want them ruined.

"She probably had a television in here," Mr. Janus said as he pointed to the empty entertainment center on the wall. His eyebrows shot up when he turned and saw Leona behind them. She nodded. "Any other electronic equipment missing?"

Leona's heart was in her stomach. She'd bought the big screen TV two years ago. The thieves had taken it and left a big gouge in the sheetrock. All of her pictures were gone from the walls and lay smashed and shattered around the room. Eggs had been thrown against the walls where their innards ran in giant streaks down toward the ruined carpet. Her kitchen knives were still stuck in the sofa, the upholstery sliced to shreds. Joe's and her recliners had suffered the same fate. The sight was too much for her heart to bear. She turned away from the scene and closed her eyes.

"Mrs. Templeton, are you okay? Let me see if I can find you someplace to sit down." Officer Torrez pushed rubble off the sofa which thudded loudly onto the floor. She pulled an afghan out from under the broken coffee table and spread it across the seat before gently guiding Leona to it. "Take a few minutes to calm down while we check out the rest of the house."

Leona stared at the floor, unwilling to look at her once immaculate home. So many thoughts swirled through her mind, she couldn't grasp one to focus on. She drew in a ragged breath, then coughed when the taste of chlorine hit her tongue. She got up and went into the kitchen.

She rubbed her temples trying to relieve the stress. *Why isn't Joe here to help me? How am I supposed to put my home back together? What kind of person would do this?*

She put her hand on the countertop, but quickly drew it back. *I don't want to touch anything that criminal touched! No telling how dirty he might have been.* She wiped her hand off on the hem of her blouse.

Out of the corner of her eye, she saw the back of her china cabinet, face-down on the floor. Pushed over by human force, glass shards lay around it. Her howl of despair brought the police officers rushing in to her aid.

"Look what they did to my treasures!" Leona wailed. She bent over and tugged at the cabinet. She was pulled away by Officer Torrez who led her back into the living room.

"Maybe it's best if you sit out on your front porch while we finish our investigation. Detective Smythe will be here soon to help us." Officer Torrez led her out the front door onto her covered front porch. Helping her sit in a big wicker chair, she said, "Have you called your insurance people yet?"

Leona shook her head.

Officer Torrez pointed to Leona's purse. "Maybe you could do that. Got your cell phone? Maybe they'll send someone out to document the damage. They'll want to get some photos for their records." She went back inside, leaving Leona alone with her cell phone.

A squeaking wheel drifted to her ear. Looking up, Leona saw Betty and Clarence coming up Joe's ramp to the front porch. Joe had put in the ramp right after he'd been diagnosed with Parkinson's. He'd known that someday he'd be unable to climb the steps and had worked hard to plan ahead for his impending disabilities.

Betty rushed up and Leona caught her arm before she could go into the house. "Stay out here with me, Betty," she said in a mournful tone. "It's too awful to see."

Betty stopped in her tracks and gasped. "I was afraid of that. What will we do? Where will we go?"

"We called the church group," Clarence said. He

lowered himself into the other wicker chair, his usual spot when visiting. He and Joe used to spend hours out there, talking about whatever old men talked about and solving the world's problems. Seeing him there made Leona miss Joe again.

Betty sat in her usual place on the porch swing and began swinging herself.

Clarence moved his walker beside his chair, clanging and banging it as he did so. Once he got it settled, he looked very satisfied with himself. "The church group should be here soon."

Leona let out a groan. "Not now, Clarence," she uttered through her clinched teeth. "I don't want to deal with them right now. Carly will come in here and tell me all the things I did wrong and what I need to do now and on and on. I can't handle that know-it-all right now."

Clarence cleared his throat as he turned to look Leona square in the face. "You need support right now. They can help you. George said he'd call his son since he knows you have homeowners insurance with him. He'll be on his way too." He turned back to sit straight in his chair. "That's one less thing you have to worry about."

Betty stopped swinging. "Speaking of calling his son, we should call our kids. They might come help us out. Diane would come."

Leona gritted her teeth. She didn't particularly care for her overbearing niece, Diane. In this situation, she'd come in and take over everything, but then so might her own daughter, Jennifer. After Joe died, Jennifer took control of all the money affairs while Leona grieved. A few months later, the two of them had gone through a power struggle over it all. Leona had to pull rank on her daughter and insist on regaining control over her own financial matters. Now this. Jennifer would fight to take back control. Leona shook her head. Not this time.

Leona raised her face to the heavens and sent a prayer

for strength. There was no escaping it. She'd have to call her kids, Jennifer and Brett, to tell them about what happened. They'd go sticking their noses into her business again.

Privacy didn't exist here. Soon the church group would crowd around her at a time when she wanted privacy to sit and cry. What she wanted most right now was to boot everyone out so she could sit in the rubble of her home with a bottle of glue. She could start to piece her things, her treasures, and her sense of normalcy back into place.

George and Irene Donovan were the first of the church group to arrive, bringing an unexpected smile to Leona's face. She loved Irene and she would help fend off Carly, the fierce she-elder, when she arrived. Between the two of them, they could handle her.

George waved as they got out of Irene's car. His heart was as large as his massive frame that had served him well during college football, but now was a detriment to his heart health. Irene was always nicely dressed, with her gray hair neatly styled to go nicely with her chunky, grandmotherly size. Her heart was as big as her husband's.

George walked up to Leona and helped her out of her chair. He gave her a side-by-side hug before going to hug Betty after she got off of the porch swing. After shaking Clarence's hand, he went into the house to look around.

"We called George Junior," Irene said as she hugged Leona. "He's on his way now. He said to tell you not to worry, your insurance policy will take care of everything."

"I hadn't even thought that far ahead," Leona said as she sat down in her wicker chair.

George walked out the house shaking his head. "Wow, they made a mess in there." Irene started to go in, but he held her back. "Stay with the ladies, please," he said softly. He walked to the end of the driveway and waved as George Junior pulled up in his large SUV. They talked together as they walked up the ramp. George Junior had taken over his father's insurance business so they spoke the same business language.

George Junior knelt down so he was face to face with Leona. He wasn't as large as his father, but he was still a tall stout man. "Mrs. Templeton, don't worry about this. You're covered. You can stay at a hotel starting tonight until we get your house back into shape. I'll take some photos to document the damage and get the paperwork started." He stood up, his knees popping as he did. "I need you to make a list of the items that were destroyed so we can submit it for reimbursement. Can you do that?"

Leona shrugged, her mind whirling. "I don't know. It's hard to say what's missing since it's such a mess."

"You don't have to do it today. Just sometime in the next week. Our policies require that we send a list in." With soft words of compassion, George Junior and George Senior went into the house.

Leona nodded, not knowing what else to do. She looked up as a long, black car parked at the curb in front of Clarence's house. A tall, lean man got out and quickly surveyed the scene and surrounding area. Dark hair, dark suit, and dark glasses, he strode toward them like a man in command of everything.

"I got here as soon as I could," he said.

Before Leona could respond, the voice of Officer Janus came from behind her. "Thanks for coming. Detective Bradley Smythe, this is Leona Templeton, the owner of the home."

The confident man nodded in her direction, taking only the ends of the fingers of her outstretched hand in his cold, limp hand. "Call me Smythe." He turned to Officer Janus and said, "Show me what you got." The two men went into the house.

Swinging on the porch swing with Irene, Betty said, "He's not overly friendly, is he?"

"I don't trust him," Leona told her friends as she rubbed her fingers to restore their warmth. "Any man who doesn't know how to properly shake someone's hand is not trustworthy. His hands were like ice and I'm pretty sure it's not because he has a warm heart."

George sat in a sturdy chair alongside Clarence. "Now Leona, don't rush to judgment. He's probably a very busy man who doesn't worry about the pleasantries."

A white Cadillac Escalade pulled up in front of the house. Before the motor was turned off, Carly Sophris got out in regal form. Being the wife of a bank president had given her an overabundance of self-importance. Dressed in black leggings and a red sparkly tunic, her dark hair and her overdone makeup made her look like an artificial life form. She always wore so much perfume that it would flash if she got too close to an open flame. Leona had to hold her breath to keep from coughing when she got too near.

Carly strutted up the ramp to the front porch like a peacock looking to impress anyone in the vicinity. Leona didn't get out of her chair as Carly tried to hug her. She had to hold her breath so she didn't get choked on the thick scent of perfume. Now she needed a shower more than ever.

"Leona, darling," Carly said as she hugged her. "My dear, I'm sorry you're going through all this. If you had a burglar alarm, it might not have happened. Smart people have burglar alarms on their houses." She made her way past the men in her high heeled sandals.

Carly's meek husband, Nick, walked onto the porch and shook everyone's hand without saying a word. A tall and distinguished-looking man, his kind manners and patient wisdom were eclipsed by his wife's overpowering presence.

Carly ceremoniously leaned against the porch railing. "You know, people like you should move into an independent living facility. This wouldn't have happened if you'd been someplace where criminals couldn't break in. This part of town is so old and it naturally draws the scum of society. You really should think about moving…"

Leona shut out the annoying sounds. She looked at her fellow sufferers on the porch. They were all looking at their shoes or hands or somewhere other than at the prattling woman leaning against the porch rail.

Detective Smythe came out on the porch, closely followed by the two police officers and George Junior. Carly kept talking until Detective Smythe put up his hand to silence her. After a few seconds, his gesture worked.

Detective Smythe stood with his feet wide and his arms crossed. "Worst burglary I've seen yet. We've had a rash of burglaries across town, but none of the others had damage as bad as this."

Carly stood and went up to face the detective, mirroring his posture. "What do you think set the thugs off, that they'd do that to Leona and Betty?"

The detective never flinched. "I don't know. I'll ask them when we catch them." He pushed his way past Carly to talk to Leona. "I'll need the same list you provide to the insurance company so we can watch for your possessions. If you have photos of any of the missing items, they would be very helpful."

Staring into his dark glasses, Leona nodded. Something about him made her uneasy, but she couldn't put her finger on exactly what that was.

"The department will keep in touch with you if we find anything." He reached inside his suit pocket and pulled out a little wallet. Taking out his business card, he handed it to Leona. "Sorry for your losses." With that, he turned on his heel and left them all looking after him as he went to his car to leave.

Officer Torrez gave Leona her business card too. "Call me when you have a list of the missing items and I'll come pick it up. Or call me if you have any questions." The two police officers left right behind the detective.

Leona stared at the business cards in her hand. She'd never forgive Joe for dying and leaving her alone to deal with things like this. She'd worked for years as a teacher, letting Joe take care of all the homeowner business matters. After he died, she had to learn the tough way how to take care of herself and her house. But she'd never had to deal with anything this complex and she didn't feel like learning something new.

George Junior waved his camera at Leona, pulling her out of her thoughts. "I've got the photos and will start your claim as soon as I get back to the office. I'll be in touch with you soon. Get a hotel room tonight and have them send the bill to me." He waved his hand toward the front door. "Don't clean this up yourself. We'll send a cleaning crew in tomorrow. Trust me, everything will be back in order before you know it."

Leona got up and gave the man a hug. "Thanks, George. I want to go through the—"she paused to find the right word, "the debris and salvage what I can. There might be something left we didn't see."

Betty walked up beside Leona. "I want to go through my room too. I had so many things in there. I don't know what I'll do if it's all gone." She teared up a little and George Junior gave her a hug.

"That's fine. Work with the crew and they'll help you sort through the debris, as you call it. I'll call you tomorrow." George Junior bid everyone good-bye and left.

Carly put her hands on her hips. "You can bet those people who clean up this place will pocket anything of value that they find. You better be here the whole time, watching them like hawks. Otherwise, they'll steal you blind." She crossed her arms and put her nose in the air.

Nick slowly got up from the step where he was sitting. "Time to go, Carly." He walked over and took her hand. Her heels clanked on the ramp as he led her away.

Carly frowned as her husband drug her toward their Escalade. "Nick, these poor women need our help! We can't go now!" She pulled her hand back, but Nick grabbed it again. She turned to look back at the front porch. "Leona. Betty. We are sorry for your loss. Let us know if we need to come help you clean up. We are available to you at any time." Nick tugged on Carly until she followed.

The others sat in silence until the large SUV pulled away. Birds in the nearby shade tree sang out a cheerful song, as if they were also happy Carly was gone. "Glad she's gone," Betty said. "Lord forgive me for talking bad about people, but she annoys me."

Clarence cleared his throat. "She annoys everybody." He pulled his walker around from the chair so it would be handy when he got up out of it. He took several swings at getting out of the low slung wicker chair. He finally got his feet under himself and pushed his walker down the porch. "I think it's time we took a look inside for ourselves."

3

Leona and the others tiptoed into the ruined living room. Betty let out a cry of despair and Clarence squeaked his way to her side. Leona was having enough trouble keeping her emotions under control that she had no strength left to comfort her sister.

After taking stock of the damage in the living room and kitchen, Leona crept down the hallway, peering into Betty's bedroom and her bath along the way. Betty's normally spotless room had been ransacked. Her clothes were scattered everywhere and the drawers of her wooden chest were thrown on the bed. Betty stood in the doorway, too stunned to enter farther. Irene and George stayed with her as Leona went on down the hallway to her own bedroom. Clarence followed close behind her.

At the door of the master suite, she looked inside and her heart nearly quit beating. Her mother's bureau had been emptied and the drawers were flung across the room. One appeared to be broken, with the side of the drawer sticking out at a funny angle.

"Oh my word! No!" she cried as she pawed through the clutter and mess on her bed. She found the small drawer from the top of the bureau underneath some clothes and shoes. Its contents had been emptied on the bed and rummaged through. Her mother's jewelry was gone. All of the jewelry was gone. The things Leona most wanted to be there were gone. She let out a distraught howl and began to cry.

Clarence was soon by her side. "What is it, dear?" Clarence said soothingly while he stroked her arm.

"They're gone! Oh, I can't believe it!" Leona covered her face with her hands. "My most prized possessions are gone!" She picked up one of her blouses off the bed and sobbed into it. Unwilling to believe what she'd found, she wiped her eyes and looked again.

She went to the bed and looked among the disheveled sheets and the drawer contents scattered on the bed. She got on the floor and felt along the carpet by the side and under the bed. Nothing. She sat back and clutched her aching heart. Joe's wedding ring was gone. A sob made its way past the lump in her throat and another cry of anguish escaped her lips. That ring was most precious to her. It was her last link to Joe.

"Are you having a heart attack?" She looked up to see Clarence leaning over his walker, peering down at her with worried eyes. He pulled his cell phone out of his pocket. "I'll call 911."

Leona reached up and put her hand over his phone. "No, I'm not having an attack."

Betty, Irene, and George hurried into the room. Betty gently nudged her sister to get up off the floor and sit on the edge of the bed. "Did they get Mama's necklace?" Leona nodded without looking at her. "Oh no! Not Mama's ruby necklace!" Betty sat beside her sister and sobbed along with her.

When the crying subsided, Leona wiped her eyes with her hands. Irene got toilet paper out of the bathroom. She handed some to both of her friends, but kept a small piece to wipe her own eyes.

Embarrassed for her friends to see her like that, Leona hurried into the master bath and looked in the mirror. Her mascara had run down her face and she looked like something from a zombie poster. Looking around, she found an unopened package of face wipes and took one out to clean up.

Irene stood in the doorway, her eyes red around the bottom. "What can I do for you, Leona?"

Leona shook her head. "Nothing. I'm over the shock and ready to get to work."

The other couple in the church group, Darren and May Bestle, came shortly after Nick and Carly left. They joined the others in with making a plan to sort through the mess. Darren and George set about making some semblance of order out the chaos. The unbroken items, like pots and pans, were set on the countertop. They needed a good washing, but other than that, were in good shape. Her 30-year-old Tupperware bowls were all there except for two lids that were probably missing before the burglary.

Clarence went home and found a spiral notebook to use to make the list that George Junior and Smythe wanted. He followed Leona around as she listed off the things she saw missing or damaged in the living room. The TV was gone. Her old turntable was gone, along with some of the old records she'd kept from years gone by. Her VCR was still there, but likely didn't work. It had been used to make the hole in the sheetrock where the TV had been. Many of the VHS tapes had the tape pulled out and tangled together.

Leona insisted the men leave the china cabinet as it was. The only unbreakable things in it were the tablecloths. Everything else was likely broken to smithereens. No, she told them, it's too late to save anything. Let the cleaning crew use their backs to move it.

She and George were making progress until she remembered Betty. She told him to sit on the sofa and check his notes while she hurried down the hall to her sister's room and looked in. Betty was picking up her clothes and hanging them up.

"Stop!" Leona cried out.

"What?" Betty said. "We've got to clean up. I can't stand this mess!"

"You're hanging up clothes that the thieves had their hands on. My word, sister, at least wash them before you put those filthy things back in your closet."

"On my clothes?" Betty looked horrified. "Eww! I didn't think about those horrible people touching my clothes! We need to wash everything." She threw her blouse across the room and held out her hand like it had been bitten. She rushed into the bathroom and washed her hands.

An hour later, the kitchen tabletop had been cleared and wiped clean by Irene and May. Everyone sat around the table talking about what needed to be done and making a plan of attack.

Leona rubbed her eyes, hoping to ease the fatigue headache that was pounding in her head. The urge to shower was almost overwhelming, but she had nothing to put on afterwards. She felt more tired than she'd felt in a long time. She offered a silent prayer. Help me get through this, Lord.

George wrote in the spiral notebook. "You need a list of all that's missing. This is the list I have so far. The TV, the record player, silverware, your computer, your mother's ruby necklace, and Joe's gold wedding band. Most of your food stock has been destroyed so I'm putting that on the list. Add photos of the missing items if you have them." George pushed the spiral notebook across the table toward Leona.

She looked through the list quickly, not really caring about it at the moment. She forced her brain to consider what needed to be done. "I have a photo of my mother with the necklace on, but who knows where it is in in this mess. I didn't take photos of my TV or things like that," Leona explained. "Does anyone?"

Clarence cleared his throat and readjusted his seat. "I've read that you should video your house so if it gets robbed, you have documentation of your possessions. I did that quite some time ago. I probably should do it again."

"George Junior had us do that several years ago," said George.

May looked at Darren. "Maybe we should do that, honey."

Leona glanced out her kitchen window. The afternoon sun was fading outside as evening came toward them. When darkness came, she didn't want to be in the shambles of her house. Creepy feelings started sliding up her arm. She didn't have much time to find something to wear, go by the pharmacy to get replacement medications, and find a hotel room. She suddenly stood up, "Let's go. We've done all we can do here for today."

May, Darren, Irene, and George left to go home, promising to come back and help more the next day. Leona scurried off to her room to take one last look, for something, but she didn't know what. Her prescription medicines were gone and she wouldn't wear any of these clothes ever again. She quickly turned and left.

Two days later, Leona and Betty sat in front of Smythe's cluttered desk. Wanting to go right to the top, Leona had decided not to call Officer Torrez, but as she sat there, she wished she had. Smythe left her feeling unsettled, like something in him wasn't right.

Smythe read over the list that the ladies had provided to him, then flipped it casually onto his file-folder laden desk. He leaned back in his office chair, tapping his fingertips together. "Thanks for the list. We'll contact all the pawnshops to watch for a ruby necklace and a worn gold wedding band. Maybe they'll turn up there, but don't hold your breath. Any items with gold or silver or other valuable minerals are usually quickly sold and melted down."

Leona gasped in panic. "Then speed is of the utmost importance. Get your men on it right away!"

Betty grabbed the arms of the chair. "Oh, yes! Let's track those criminals down!"

Smythe's eyebrows raised as he looked down his nose at them. He waved his hand toward his piles of files on his desk. "See these? Cases. Unsolved cases. You're not the only one in town with a problem. We can't concentrate manpower on just a necklace and a ring." He paused, closed his eyes, and quickly clenched and unclenched his fists. "We'll do all we can to recover your things."

Leona leaned forward and tapped on a pile of folders. "You telling us that we're low priority? We're tax payers, you know. We've been paying taxes since before you were born. I think we deserve a little more consideration."

Smythe's eyes narrowed. "We'll work with the local pawnshops and keep an eye out for your things. That's the best we can do."

"That's not enough!" Leona stood up and glared at the detective across his desk. He had a droopy-eyed look of boredom on his face, indicating he didn't have the time or patience to deal with her.

"The matter is under investigation. We're doing all we can." He shuffled a few of the papers on his desk, dismissing her.

"I know the police chief. All of his kids were in my classes. He knows who I am." The words came out louder than Leona had intended. Betty reached out to take Leona's arm to calm her. Leona pushed it away.

The detective slammed his hands on his desk and rose over it. "The chief knows about the burglary. He knows we're investigating it. He knows it's an active case. He knows we don't have the manpower to go door-to-door looking for your stolen TV set. He's as sorry as he can be that you have to miss your game shows and soap operas, but we'll let you know if anything turns up. Now..." he stood up, straightening his tall frame a little higher and shouted, "...go away! I have work to do!" He plopped into his chair behind his desk and opened a file folder and started reading.

"Well, I never!" Leona exclaimed as she stomped her foot. "A public servant treating a taxpayer that way!"

"Come on, Leona." Betty pulled at her sister. "Thank you for your time, Mr. Smythe." She kept pulling on Leona who seemed rooted to the spot. "It's time to go home now, Leona." She gave one last tug and Leona moved with her.

"I'll be back!" Leona yelled over her shoulder as they went out the door.

"Keep your voice down, Leona." Betty tried to soften Leona's anger as they made their way back to the foyer where Clarence waited for them. "Throwing a fit isn't going to make them work any harder."

"But it makes me feel better!" Leona stomped her foot again.

Clarence stood up as he saw them approaching. "How'd it go?"

Leona growled in response and stomped her feet in frustration.

Betty pulled away from Leona, letting her continue with her angry show. "They're investigating. That's all they'll say."

"Let them do their jobs," Clarence pushed his walker against Leona. "They'll find your things. Don't worry." He kept nudging her along toward the door.

Betty came by her and took her by the elbow to nudge her along. Clarence's walker squeaked its way behind them. The trio slowly made their way down the sidewalk. Hopelessness filled Leona so fully that she stopped to turn around and look back at the entry door of the police station. She was tempted to go back in and give Smythe a good lecture.

Clarence reached out to take Leona's arm and bring her along with him and Betty. "Leona dear, the police will do all they can. Don't worry."

Leona jerked her arm away. "I'm not your dear! They don't care about my mother's necklace or Joe's ring. They don't understand that those things are all I have left of them. All that I have left that touched them." Her voice broke as she despaired.

Betty put her arms around Leona's waist and squeezed. "Don't worry, Leona. I have a plan. Remember how in that TV show Murder She Wrote, Jessica Fletcher took matters into her hands? Why don't we go investigate like she did when someone was murdered? Just ask a few questions and put the pieces of the puzzle together. Just like those jigsaw puzzles we work on."

Leona shook her head. "That's TV. This is reality. Let's just go home." She walked wearily down the sidewalk toward the minivan.

"No, really!" Betty called after her. "If the police won't do it, we can!"

4

"You missed our turn!" Betty said as Leona drove the minivan down the street.

"We're not going home yet," Leona replied as she stopped at a red light. "I'm going to see Ernie about what I can do."

"Ernie?" Clarence leaned forward from the backseat. "Why Ernie?"

"But what about my plan?" Betty was almost frantic. "We can do this ourselves! We don't need Matlock to solve it for us. That would take all our fun away." She sat back in her seat pouting.

When they came to another stoplight, Leona glanced over at her pouting sister, sitting there in her new outfit. The two of them had visited the Penney store this morning and picked up a few nice blouses and some polyester pants, plus the requisite unmentionables.

Leona turned back to watching the light. "My house was robbed and I think I should see a lawyer about it. Maybe he can help get the ball rolling on the investigation. I could threaten a lawsuit." She could feel her anger rising. "The police should have kept us safe from hoodlums! Why, what if we'd been home when they came? We might be dead if it hadn't been for Al's funeral!"

Betty cried out in alarm. "Dead? Oh my! Al saved us by dying. What a wonderful man! He saved us from being murdered!" She started to get weepy and dug in her purse for tissues.

"That's ridiculous!" Clarence reached past the seat back to pat Betty's shoulders. "We wouldn't have been murdered. The burglars wouldn't have come if you'd been home. Now there, there." He barked at Leona, "Tell her you didn't mean it!"

"Hush now, Betty," Leona said more softly, reaching over to pat her arm. "I was just being melodramatic. I'm sorry I upset you."

"But it could be true. We might have been killed for our clothes and TV set if we'd been home. Oh sweet, sweet Al. He saved us from being murdered!"

Leona looked toward heaven for help and said a prayer. In doing so, she missed the light turning green. The car behind them tapped the horn, signaling that her prayer had taken too long. She frowned in the rearview mirror and drove on as Betty sniffled and wiped her eyes.

"Stop crying, Betty! I forgot how gullible you are. I just made up the murder part. Forget I said it." She reached over to pat her sister's hand again. "I'm going to see Ernie to get advice on what to do. I have to get my things back. Maybe he has an idea. If not, we always have your plan."

The trio stood in front of the receptionist's desk in the lawyer's office in the antiquated office building. The office seemed dated, with the tired country blue décor. The young receptionist behind the desk was wearing a blouse that was too low in the front and a skirt that was too high all the way around. She stared at them like her mind was on vacation elsewhere.

"What do you mean he's not here anymore?" Leona

asked, hoping to stir some sign of brain activity in her face. "Ernie's been here for over 30 years. How could he up and leave without saying anything? He's the lawyer I use for everything."

The young lady shook her head. "Mr. Lanyard's been gone for several months." She glanced around nervously before staring at Leona. "Um—when he found out he had cancer and didn't have much time left, he moved to be near his daughter in Cleveland. He sold his office and his practice to Tristan—er, my boss, Mr. Wilcox."

Leona crossed her arms. "But why didn't someone inform me of this? Ernie's been my lawyer for years. I should have been informed about what's going on."

"We've only been open a few days and we haven't made it through all the files left behind. What did you say your name was?" She started digging through a pile of file folders on her desk.

"Templeton. Leona Templeton."

The young thing sat back in her chair. "That explains it. We're only up to L in the files. I think T comes after that."

Leona fumed. "As a former teacher, I can assure you that T does indeed come after L." She turned to look at her companions. "Did you know anything about this?" Both of them shook their heads, so she turned back to the young lady. "What happened to Paula, Ernie's secretary?"

The young lady shrugged and avoided eye contact. "She retired, I think. All I know is that I have the job now. Is there something you want?"

Leona turned to look at her companions with disgust and a roll of her eyes. "Oh my word. Now what do I do?"

"Talk to Tristan." Betty smiled as she said it. "He's a lawyer too. Right, Miss?" They turned to look at the young lady.

"Oh yes, I've seen his diploma. He's a lawyer all right."

Leona smiled at the young thing. "Then I'd like to see him, if you please."

"He's not in right now—"

A man's voice sounded behind them. "Hello!" A young man walked in and closed the door behind him. Dressed in a cheap suit with his tie folded and hanging out of his pocket, he extended his hand. "Oh, I didn't know anyone but Amber was here. Are you clients of Mr. Lanyard? I'm Tristan Wilcox. I'm taking over his practice." He shook hands with all three of them when they told him their names. "Why don't you come into my office and let's talk. Amber, can you get some bottled water for these folks?" He opened his office door and motioned for them to come in.

Leona didn't immediately move. Ernie was an old friend of Joe's and she trusted him. He had years of experience in handling whatever she and Joe brought to him. But this kid? What did he know? He was probably just out of law school with no experience to do anything. She fought the urge to turn and leave.

Tristan motioned again for them to come. Betty nudged Leona from behind. Leona let out a soft sigh and went inside the office. It looked the same as when Ernie was there, with a large, carved wooden desk and an oversized chair behind it. A matching wooden table stood in front of a wall covered in reference books on wooden bookshelves. The tan carpet, to Leona's surprise, seemed threadbare. When Ernie was handling Joe's matters after his death, she'd thought Ernie kept a nice office. She must have been too preoccupied or too bereaved to notice how old everything seemed.

Tristan pulled a chair from the table to set beside the two chairs in front of the desk and took his seat behind his desk. He folded his hands together. "I've only been here a couple of weeks and haven't had time to review all of the files. Were you clients of Mr. Lanyard? Was there an issue he was working on for you?"

"Ernie was an old friend of my husband's," Leona

began. "I need advice in a matter and thought he might help me. I hear he's not here anymore."

Tristan shook his head. "He had to leave town suddenly and well, here I am."

Betty sadly shook her head. "The young lady told us he had cancer and didn't have long to live." She found a tissue in her purse and wiped her eyes.

Tristan got an amused look on his face. "Yes. Well, that's the story..." His voice trailed off.

"Why didn't Nancy let us know about Ernie?" Betty looked inquisitive. "Poor Nancy. What will she do without Ernie?"

"Trust me, she'll do fine," Tristan said. He leaned forward, his chair creaking with his movement. He whispered. "Were you really good friends?"

Leona lifted her eyebrows in surprise. "We all sort of grew up together here. We're all hometown folks. Why do you ask?"

Tristan chuckled again and whispered, "He doesn't have cancer. He ran off to Mexico with his secretary. His wife is the one who moved to Cleveland to be near their daughter." He sat back with a big grin on his face.

The trio sat back in their chairs with their mouths hanging open. Clarence leaned forward and spoke for the three of them, "Ernie ran off with Paula?" He started laughing, hard, like a man envious of another man's victory. "That Ernie! Who knew he had a thing for Paula? They'd been working together almost as long as he'd been married." He went into another spate of laughing.

Leona slapped her hand on the desk which made Clarence stop his snickering for a moment. "Clarence Brown, you're laughing about a man who deserted his wife and is living in sin. That's not funny! It's shameful!"

Clarence choked down his amusement and agreed with her.

Betty jumped in. "So Nancy's all right? She's being

seen to by their daughter? I'm glad she's in Cleveland. It would be hard to face anyone around here after what Ernie did."

Tristan, still smiling from watching Clarence, answered, "She sold me his practice lock, stock, and barrel. For a good price, I might add. I was happy to walk into an established practice. Other than getting acquainted with everyone, I hope things will stay just the way they were when Ernie was here."

Clarence cleared his throat. "If you want some advice from me, you might look for better clerical help. She might be good-looking, but she's not the brightest."

Tristan laughed. "She's my cousin who wanted to earn a little money before going to beauty school. I'll advertise for a real law clerk when I can afford one. Now, what can I do for you?"

Leona moved up to the front of her chair. "I'm the one with the problem. My house was robbed and I don't think the police are doing all they can to find my things. I wanted to know if you could make them search harder."

Tristan frowned while he mulled it over. "What do the police tell you they are doing?"

"Investigating." Leona felt antsy and started to rise, but then decided to stay sitting. "That's it. They're not rousting criminals or talking to their informants or..."

"How do you know they're not?"

"They haven't found my things yet."

"These things take time." Tristan leaned forward in his chair. "How long has it been since the robbery?"

Betty blurted out, "Two days."

Tristan's eyebrows shot up. "Two days? That's not much time. Investigations may take a while. Maybe they don't have any suspects so they have to look at all aspects of the crime. Oh, sometimes they solve it sooner, but I think tracking down burglars takes longer than two days."

"The detective told me that thieves sell gold jewelry and

then it's melted down. There's no time to lose. I need them to find them now! This 'we're investigating' is not a satisfactory answer for me."

Clarence spoke up. "The detective called it an active investigation."

Tristan nodded in understanding. "That's good. It means they're doing all they can to solve it." He looked at Leona. "Is there something in particular you want them to find?"

"My Joe's gold wedding band. It's all I have left of him and I want it back." Leona felt like she were going to cry. "And my mother's ruby necklace. I want that back too."

The door opened and the young receptionist walked in with four bottles of water. She put them on the desk and left. Tristan stood up and twisted the caps to make sure they were easier to open. He handed the bottles to his clients.

"The police are doing their jobs. I know that you may not like it, but that's probably their procedures for any burglary. The only thing you can do is wait for them to do their investigations. The necklace and the ring, they're small items, easy to hide and hard to find." He pressed his lips together. "And I'm sorry to say it, but I don't think they'll ever find them. You may need to accept that they're gone."

His words cut right through her heart. Leona rubbed her aching temples and heaved a heavy sigh. "Then there's nothing you can do to hurry it along?"

"Not really. I advise you to be patient. You could call them every few days and ask if there's been any progress. That might push them a little harder. Otherwise, you need to stay out of their way. Did you call your insurance agent?"

Leona sighed again. The lump in her throat was throbbing as much as her head was. "Yes, they are helping me with the cleanup and repairs. Yesterday I watched them carry the broken remains of my belongings out the door and put them into a dumpster." She paused to push the lump back down. "But I can't put a dollar value on things that are sentimental."

Tristan opened a drawer in his big wooden desk and pulled out a purse packet of tissues. He tossed them toward her side of the desk. The motion seemed calloused and his face reddened as he realized it. He made several awkward moves to pick them up and set them down more gently. He finally gave up and continued, "I'm very sorry for your loss. You're right. Some things can never be replaced. I don't know what else to tell you. Just say your prayers that a miracle will happen."

It wasn't the answer Leona wanted to hear, but she realized the futility of pressing the issue. She thanked him and stood to go. "Send me a bill for your time. You should find me in your files when you get to the Ts."

"No charge," Tristan said as he escorted them to the door. "I didn't do anything for you. Besides, it's nice to meet some of my clients." He cleared his throat and leaned forward. "I feel I should make this clear. I'm a corporate lawyer, not a criminal lawyer. I can help you some with the insurance issues, but I'm not sure I can be of much help regarding the criminal issues of this case."

Leona pursed her lips. "Maybe you should do some research about it." She stood and helped Clarence get to his feet. "Thanks for your time." Tristan shook their hands as they went out.

Back in the minivan, Betty said, "He's a nice young man. I think he'll make a great lawyer."

"You would," Leona said as she turned toward home. "Let's talk about that plan of yours."

5

On their way home, Betty got a call on her cell phone that several of the church group members were at her house, waiting to help clean up the mess. As Leona pulled into the driveway, she was surprised to see several people sitting on the porch. May was sitting on the porch swing with Carly. Both ladies were deep in conversation, oblivious to the men's conversations going on. May was a good person to put up with Carly like that. Nick was on the lawn under the tree talking on his cell phone. He waved to them as they drove into the driveway.

The cleaning crew minivan was parked at the curb near the large dumpster sitting in the driveway behind the Newport. The day before, the three-man crew made good progress in the clean-up, but it wasn't easy for Leona to hear the clanging noises as they threw her belongings and memories into the dumpster. She hadn't stayed long to listen. Not wanting to wear her funeral dress another day, she and Betty spent the rest of the day at the mall.

Coming down the ramp as Leona parked the minivan, Darren said, "We should have called earlier, but we assumed you'd be here cleaning up." He went to the other side of the minivan to help with Clarence's walker.

Betty rushed forward to announce to the group. "We were checking on the police to make sure they are working hard to find our things."

"And are they?" May asked as she and Carly joined the others.

"It's under investigation," Clarence stated, wheeling his squeaky walker toward the ramp.

"Active investigation," Betty added as the others came down the ramp.

"Nick can oil that squeak for you, Clarence," Carly said. She stood by the garage door, her heavy perfume filling the air around them.

"What squeak?" Clarence glared at her as he walked past.

"I don't hear anything," Darren said to her as he walked past her as well. He patted Clarence on the back as they both made their way up the ramp to the porch.

Carly looked upset. She opened her mouth to say something, but on this rare occasion, decided against it. She followed everyone else back to the porch where Leona was unlocking the new front door lock.

Leona swung the door open and told the group, "I'd ask you in for tea, but our house is a mess."

"That's why we're here!" Carly said in a singsong voice. "We're here to help get your house back in order because that's what our church group is about."

"Are George and Irene coming?" Leona asked right before her sister poked her in the ribs.

"Who cares!" Betty sang out. "We'll take all the help we can get. Come on in here. We can make some coffee in our new coffee pot. We got it just this morning. I think there's still a few cookie tins in the freezer. They went through our freezer in the house, but didn't get into our freezer in the garage. Thank goodness for that! We have a few things left. "

"And that's where you keep your cold hard cash, no

doubt," Nick added. The group chuckled at the less-than-clever pun out of politeness.

The group entered the living room where the carpet had been stripped so the subflooring was showing. The linoleum in the kitchen was clean and the cabinets were back to their normal appearance. The house smelled of new paint.

"The crews have done a good job," Leona explained as she led the group around her home. "As you can see, they've repaired the wall damage and repainted the walls. George Junior said the crews will lay new carpet later this week. It's gone faster than I expected. We should be back in here by next week."

"How wonderful!" Carly cried out. "And you'll have new furniture and all new things. I wish our house had been robbed!" Her wide sparkling eyes looked all around the room. The group fell silent with open mouths. Nick shook his head and went into the kitchen to help Betty with the coffee.

"Did you get a list for the insurance company?" May said quietly. After Leona nodded, she added, "That must have been hard work."

Leona was grateful that May had the good sense to move the attention from Carly to something else. "Yes, we spent all day yesterday going through things. The crew threw out the broken stuff. We threw out everything else, like our clothes, towels, toiletries, and such. The thought of filthy burglars having their hands on our personal stuff—well, we just couldn't use it again. Out it went."

May nodded. "I would feel the same way. I'd rather do without a few things than use what's been soiled by sinful hands."

"Coffee's ready!" Nick and Betty walked out from the kitchen with white foam cups filled with dark liquid. "Get your fresh hot coffee and grab some cookies from the kitchen. Let's sit on the front porch out of the paint fumes."

"I'd go a thousand miles to get some of your delicious cookies, Betty," Clarence said as he squeaked his way along. Others managed to pass him and grab a cookie before he got there. With a soft cry of triumph, he picked up two.

Carly peeked in a cupboard. Her mouth fell open. She opened another cupboard and another one, banging the doors and drawers shut as she went along. "Not much in here. Did you throw it all out?"

Leona walked over to Carly and pushed the cabinet door shut. "The breakable things were broken. The other things are being sanitized. Now, stay out of my cabinets and get some coffee and cookies." Her tone of voice made Carly's eyebrows shoot up. With a soft snort, she went to join the others outside on the porch. Betty followed with the pot of coffee and the rest of the cookies.

Carly sat her odoriferous self in Leona's wicker chair. "Your old stuff was shabby. Now you can get some nice things." She took a bite of cookie.

An uncomfortable silence filled the air until Betty added, "It's easier to clean empty cabinets than full ones. Besides, we want to sanitize everything. There's no telling what kind of germs have been left behind by those…those criminals. We got buckets and bleach at the store this morning, but we left them in the back of the minivan. May, can you help me get those?"

Nick put down his coffee cup. "Carly and I will get them. Come on, Carly." At first, Carly sat there with a look of determination on her face. Nick took her arm and pulled her out of the chair and down the ramp out of sight, far enough away that the others never heard any sound from them after they left.

The members of the church group who remained on the porch stared at each other. One of them let out a snicker and the others joined in, muffling their laughter as best as they could.

"What I wouldn't give to hear that conversation!" Darren whispered. May gave him a playful slap on the arm.

"The wood shed's out back," Clarence added. "That's where we had to go when we were rude to people."

Leona agreed with him. "The only reason to put up with her is for Nick's sake. He's such a sweet man and so eager to help. It would break his heart to be excluded because he's married to a belligerent woman." She snapped her fingers trying to kick start her memory. "What's that verse in Proverbs?"

Darren provided the answer. "'Better to dwell in the wilderness, than with a contentious and angry woman.'"

"Poor Nick!" Leona said, trying not to laugh. "I bet he wishes he lived in the wilderness right now."

"Shhh, here they come." Betty started refilling coffee cups while the rest of them picked up small conversation amongst themselves and raved about the treats, acting like they hadn't noticed anything out of the ordinary.

Carly and Nick walked by with the cleaning supplies, going straight into the house. Leona and Betty followed them. Nick put the buckets in the sink and filled them with hot bleach water. Leona opened a new package of sponges and put them in the water.

"Who's up for cleaning?" Leona wrung out the sponges and offered them to any volunteer.

Carly stepped up and said, "Nick and I have to go. Sorry to bug out on the work, but I have an appointment that I can't miss. Come on, Nick." She turned on her heel and left.

Nick's face reddened and he fumbled with his baseball cap. "We have to go. Leona, should I come back in a little bit to help?"

Leona smiled at the poor man and gave him a wink. "No, the four of us can handle it. You have your hands full."

He gave her a crooked grin and nodded before leaving.

He leaned close to Leona's ear and whispered, "I wish I was in the wilderness!" He left the others, laughing as he went out.

When Nick was safely out of earshot, Betty asked, "What did he tell you?"

Leona's face contorted with barely controlled laughter. "He either heard us talking or he's thinking the same thing we are. He wishes he were in the wilderness."

Their laughter brought the painting contractors out to see what was going on. Betty offered them the remainder of her cookies before their supervisor sent them back to work.

May stepped up and took one of the sponges. "I'll start in the bathroom." She picked up a bucket of bleach water and whistled a lively tune as she went down the hallway.

After two hours of scrubbing and sanitizing, the house smelled like bleach and fresh paint. Betty insisted the refrigerator be totally emptied since she didn't know whether the burglars had touched what was left in the vegetable drawer and "contaminated it" or if it was safe to eat. When evening came around, the sponges were in the trash can along with the salad makings from the refrigerator.

In appreciation for their help, Leona and Betty took Clarence, May, and Darren out for dinner. Still in their work clothes, they ended up at Whataburger. The food was good, but the group was so tired that none of them lingered too long. On the way to take Clarence home, Betty hummed hymns as she smiled and waved at passersby.

"You're certainly in a good mood," Clarence remarked from the backseat. "Happy to see your house getting back in order?"

Betty nodded. "Things are looking up. The kitchen and bathrooms are clean and ready to be used. The living room looks almost like it did. Once we get the new furniture, the house will be good as new. And wasn't it nice of the church group to come help us out? Isn't fellowship a wonderful thing?"

Clarence agreed. "Leona, you don't seem very happy."

Leona growled lowly. "Mother's necklace and Joe's ring are still missing. I want them back. They're MINE!" She hit the steering wheel with her fist. "I told Joe I'd pass his ring along to Brett. I must keep my word to him."

"You should have given it to him after Joe died, just like I told you to!" Betty sounded gruff, her good attitude ruined by Leona's anger.

Leona turned her head to yell at Betty, "You don't understand!" Looking back at the road, she slammed on the brakes as she passed a stop sign. The screech of tires and the sight of a car coming from her left made her scream in fright. The car seemed impossibly close as it ground to stop in front of her. The driver in the car joined her in a scream, his seen but not heard. His lips formed vile words as he shrieked at her from behind his windshield. Leona yelled an apology, hoping he could hear her or at least lip read what she said. The man drove away after shaking his fist at her.

Her stunned passengers said nothing as she pulled up to the curb across the intersection. She laid her head on the steering wheel and sobbed. "I put—" Leona said softly between sobs as Betty handed her several tissues, "the ring on Joe's pillow—" she blew her nose, "I put his ring on his pillow at night. It made me feel like he was there with me." She quietly sobbed into a tissue. "How can I sleep not knowing where it is?" She sobbed again.

Betty's tears were running fast down her face. "Oh, my dear sister," she sobbed as she leaned across as far as her seatbelt would allow and tried to put her arm around Leona. "I had no idea." The sisters cried together, joined in occasionally by soft sniffling from the backseat.

A rap at the window pulled them all back out of their crying jag. Six teary eyes peered out the window at the starched uniform of a police officer. Leona rolled the window down. "Yes, sir?"

"Ma'am, we got a report of a minivan running this stop sign. Would that be you?"

Leona squinted at the middle aged officer, then at his name badge. "Hey, weren't you in my class?"

The officer tilted his head as he looked closely at her. "Mrs. Templeton?"

"Oh, thank goodness, one of my students is here!" She patted her chest to calm her heart down. "We are so distressed! I stopped just a little too far past the stop sign and this car zoomed in front of us and the man screamed at us! He used terrible words and we were so upset by the whole episode that I had to pull over while we cried." Only a small white lie. The officer wouldn't understand her emotions over Joe's ring. For effect, Leona wiped her eyes.

The officer fumbled with his pen and reached out to pat Leona on the shoulder. "I don't mean to upset you more, but we have to investigate the call complaining about someone running a stop sign. Your minivan matches the description we were given and he said that an older woman was driving. So I have to ask you again, did you run that stop sign and nearly hit a car?"

"Technically, I stopped for the sign. I just didn't see it in time to stop in the right place."

"Technically, it's still called running a stop sign."

Leona conceded defeat. "Okay, write me a ticket then." She sniffled and wiped her nose. "Betty, hand me the registration to the minivan."

Betty's hands shook as she opened the glove box and fumbled around looking for the plastic folder holding the registration. "Oh Officer, don't be too harsh with her. She's upset about our house being robbed and they took her husband's wedding ring. Did you know that she puts it—"

"Betty!" Leona yelled, "This nice officer doesn't have time to listen to our woes. Just get the registration."

The officer leaned down and looked in. "I heard about the robbery. I feel bad about it. There've been a lot of burglaries in the area in the past year. We're all keeping an eye out for suspicious activity."

"An active investigation," Leona muttered under her breath.

The officer leaned closer. "Pardon? I didn't catch that?"

"She asked if you've rounded up suspects yet," Clarence asked from the back.

The officer leaned down so he could see Clarence. "No sir, I don't think we have any suspects yet. We're running extra patrols and keeping our ears to the ground."

"Is that all?" Leona demanded. "You're not raiding known dens of thieves and hoodlums?"

The officer chuckled lightly. "Not today. I hope we find whoever did it." He took her license and registration before starting to write on his pad. He gave it to her to sign. "I'm going to let you off with just a warning today, Mrs. Templeton, because I know the robbery upset you. In the future, watch out for stop signs and stop behind the line. Be safe out here."

"Thank you. I'll be more careful." Leona was relieved at being let go. "Nice to see you again. Keep up the good work," she said half-heartedly.

6

"What are you doing?" Betty asked while she was cleaning up the containers of their microwaved oatmeal breakfast. Since they were still in an extended-stay hotel room, they were cooking in the microwave, eating off of paper plates, and drinking coffee from disposable cups.

"I'm making a list of places to go shopping today. George called this morning. The insurance company has issued a check for the replacement of our dishes, TV, and other things that were taken. I'll call Jennifer later and ask her to order a new computer for us. She knows more about them than I do."

Betty wiped the very small countertop in the kitchenette. "Let's get the TV first. I miss my programs."

"It's at the top of my list. But first, I thought we could start checking out the pawnshops for Mother's necklace. I'm making a list of them to visit."

Betty wrinkled her nose. "Pawnshops? Aren't those kind of seedy places to go?"

"I don't know. I've never been to one, but I'm not going to sit here and do nothing while the police 'increase patrols' and other ineffective things." Leona closed the phone book and looked at her list. "That's all that are listed there. My goodness, who knew we had so many pawnshops spread across town."

A light knock at the door told them that the cleaning woman had arrived for her morning chores. Betty yelled out to come in and turned to get another disposable cup for her coffee. Never offend the person doing the cleaning, Betty had said when they'd first arrived. So they offered her coffee every day, whether she cleaned their room or not.

Leona looked up from the small dining table when she realized no one had come in. Betty gave her a questioning look. She went to the door and opened it, but it wasn't the cleaning lady standing there. Smythe, in a business suit, was standing in the doorway

"Oh! It's you!" Betty said as Leona spun around and let out a frightened squeal.

Smythe took a step inside the doorway. "I'm sorry to barge in on you like this. Mr. Brown told me you were here."

Leona covered her heart with her hand. "You scared us! We thought you were the cleaning lady here for coffee. She stops by every morning to visit for a few minutes. Please come in." Waving an invitation to him, she pointed to the small sofa in the corner. Betty set down the coffee cup in front of him before sitting in the other chair.

Leona stared at Smythe as he looked around the room. Under different circumstances, she'd think he was a handsome young man. He dressed well, was neatly groomed and clean-shaven, and seemingly well mannered. On the outside, he looked like someone she might consider introducing to her oldest granddaughter, but her gut told her that something about him was amiss. The outside of him was a disguise for something dark and sinister on the inside.

She pushed the feeling away. After all, he was looking for her stuff. "What brings you here today?"

He made a sound of approval after he tasted Betty's coffee. Loosening his coat button, he turned to Leona. "I was gruff with you yesterday and I wanted to apologize. I'd had a bad day, but that's no excuse for what I said. And I stopped by to answer any other questions you might have."

Leona lightly tapped her pen on the table. "Have you found anything yet?"

"Um, this coffee is a lot better than the stuff at the office." He took another sip. "No, we haven't found anything yet, but we're hopeful. I know you are particularly interested in finding a ruby necklace and a gold wedding band, right?"

Betty jumped in. "The thieves took our mother's ruby necklace and her late husband's gold wedding band. Poor Leona has been despondent over the loss of those items. Do you know what she does with that ring? It will break your heart!"

"Betty!" Leona said a little too loudly. "The detective isn't interested in those trivial stories. He's a busy man. Aren't you."

He nodded as he sipped more coffee. "Yes, this is mighty fine coffee. You even have the same china pattern that we have at the office." He chuckled at his own attempt at humor, but Leona was not amused.

Leona forced a faked smile on her face. "Betty has quite a knack for making good coffee. And good cookies. Once we move back home, she can start to cook in a proper kitchen and restock her cookie supplies and such." She eyed him to see if he would react. He didn't. "Are you hot on the trail of the culprits?"

He clinched his fist slightly and worked a muscle in his jaw. "We're doing the best we can. As I told you, there's been a rash of burglaries around town in the past year. We think there's a well-organized burglary ring that we're having trouble finding. But we'll get them. Wait and see."

Leona watched his fists get tighter and the jaw muscle

was working harder. He seemed more intent on the coffee than most people would have been. *I think I'm getting under his skin.* She watched him swallow hard. His features softened and appeared under control again.

"And what about my ruby necklace and gold band?"

"Everything on your list can be easily disposed of. The small items like your jewelry disappear quickly because they're so easily hidden, traded, or sold. Or melted down for their precious metals content. Like I told you yesterday, there's a good chance we'll never find them."

Leona's brain froze on hearing those words again. Melted down! The ring would be gone forever. Just like Joe. She would have to face his loss every night, alone in that empty bed. With the empty pillow beside her. She couldn't bear to think of it. Her heart felt heavy which made it hard for her to breathe. She felt a soft touch on her shoulder and looked into the face of her sister.

Betty was looking at her. "Mr. Smythe asked you a question, dear."

Leona blinked away the moisture gathered in her eyes. "I'm sorry, what did you say?"

Smythe looked at her puzzled. "I said I stopped by to see if you had serial numbers we could track. On your TV and computer." He looked at her expectantly.

"Serial numbers? I don't know. Let me think a minute." Leona pushed her worries from her mind. "We have the operation manuals somewhere. I'll look for those when we stop back by the house."

"That would help us out," Smythe said. "If they show up in a pawnshop, we'll know who took them in."

"Are you looking through pawnshops?"

The disposable cup he set down had an indentation around it where his hand had been. His hand movements became slower and more deliberate. "Rarely do they show up there because pawnshop owners require proof that the person bringing the item in is the owner. They take photos and submit information to us to compare against the stolen goods list. Even then, not a lot of stolen merchandise goes through the pawnshops. Most stolen items are sold through the black market."

Betty piped up. "Black market? Here? I thought they only had those in third world countries." She leaned across the table toward him. "I've always wondered, are there other colors of markets?"

The clock on the wall counted off the seconds of silence. Leona stared at Betty, wondering what prompted such a silly question. Smythe sat still, open-mouthed. He folded his hands together. "As far as I know, there're no other colors of illegal markets. The black market can be anywhere. All it takes is a man on the street opening his coat and asking if you want to buy one of the stolen watches he has hanging in it."

"I thought they were called flashers?"

Leona slammed her hands down on the table. "Never mind! Let's not go there. Do you need anything else, Smythe?"

Smythe fought to hide a grin. "No, this will help us. I'll be in touch. Ladies, thanks for the coffee. It was delicious." Leona held the door for him as he left.

Leona leaned against the door and looked at Betty. "I wonder what his *real* reason was for coming."

"Why are we driving here?" Clarence asked in the whiny high-pitched voice of a child wanting to go out to play. "Smythe said they're checking the pawnshops."

"I'm helping the police out," Leona said, her hands firmly gripping the wheel. Smythe's visit that morning had spurred her to action. His continual talk of taking care of things and ongoing investigations convinced her that he wanted her to believe it, but he wasn't actually doing it.

She pulled into a parking lot beside a seedy-looking pawnshop. The bars over the windows and fading paint didn't give a come-on-in look to the place. Litter of all sorts lay along the foundation of the building and against the fence in the back. The grungy look of the lone person smoking beside an Employees-Only side door put her off, but nothing would keep her from her mission. Finding a spot near the door, the stopped and told Betty and Clarence, "Stay here to make sure nothing else gets stolen. I'll be right back."

"Do hurry!" Betty cried out just before the door slammed.

Leona smoothed her new polyester slacks and blouse and felt her hair to make sure it was in place. Her heart was beating fast as she opened the door and stepped inside. To her surprise, the interior was clean and neat, in stark contrast to the exterior. A multitude of musical instruments lined one wall, with electronic equipment displayed inside the glass case in front of them. In the middle of the room, diamond jewelry sparkled under the fluorescent lights in another glass case. On the other end of the store, guns of all makes and calibers lined the wall and display case. Bicycles, power tools, and a myriad of items were lined up in front of the big windows at the front of the store and along the aisles toward the back.

A lady behind the jewelry counter called out, "May I help you, ma'am?" She gave Leona a good customer-service smile.

Walking to the display case, Leona's eyes were drawn to the sparkling diamonds of the many wedding ring sets in the case. Scanning for anything familiar, she replied, "I'm looking for a necklace of mine that was stolen from my house several days ago."

Silence filled the store as everyone turned to look at her. A frown replaced the smile on the clerk's face. She replied loudly enough for all to hear, "We don't accept stolen items in this store. We work closely with the police department to make sure none of our items are hot."

The man behind the gun counter came up beside the clerk with narrowed eyes that left no doubt that he wouldn't allow such rumors to spread. "Who told you we sell stolen goods?"

Leona felt her face redden, and her racing heart urged her to turn and run. She looked down to see her shuffling feet, then looked the man. "No one! I didn't mean to imply that you did. I'm acting out of desperation to find something precious to me, and I didn't know where else to look. The police said they were checking pawnshops and I thought I'd help them out."

The man's eyes relaxed a little. "We work with the police, not private citizens. I suggest you go home so you don't bother our customers."

Leona took a step back. "I'm sorry, I didn't mean to imply anything untoward about your business. I apologize if I did." Leona studied the man's face. Less hostility seemed to be there so she took another chance before he kicked her out for good. She leaned in closer to him and spoke softly. "Maybe you can still help me. Can you tell me about a place where I might find stolen items? Is there a black marketplace that I might visit?"

Snickers around the store told Leona she'd asked a silly question in too loud of a whisper. She apologized again. "Look, the thieves took my mother's necklace and my late husband's wedding band. I must get them back, and I didn't know where else to look. I—I should have never come here." She turned to go with what little dignity she had left.

"Wait!" the man called after her.

Leona stopped. She closed her eyes as she tried to decide whether to stay to listen or keep going. Betty and Clarence were impatiently sitting in the minivan, wondering about her no doubt. But what other chance might she have to get information? Reaching a decision, she opened her eyes and turned around.

The man drummed his fingers on the glass counter.

"Come back. We can go talk in my office. Darcie, you and Jason take over for a few minutes." He held his arm out to direct her way.

Whispering and soft giggling followed Leona to the office door. She entered a neat but small office in the back of the shop. Papers with lists, sticky notes, and posters of guns wallpapered the office walls. Two filing cabinets filled an already small space behind the desk. She took a seat in the folding chair in the corner. Her knees brushed against the front of the desk as she sat there.

The man sat behind the desk and looked at her, not unkindly, but like a man who didn't know what to do with her. "Ever been in a pawnshop before?"

Leona shook her head.

"I didn't think so. Listen, Mrs.—"

"Templeton. Leona Templeton."

"Mrs. Templeton. You seem confused so I'll be straight with you. Us pawnshop dealers work hard to stay within the law. We're not criminals. We're businessmen trying to run our business so we can support our families. We work closely with police when they're looking for stolen goods. Here, I'll show you." He pulled a desk drawer open and pulled out a pile of papers. "Here's a list of what they're looking for." He flipped through the stack, then handed a few to her to examine. She quickly scanned the photos and descriptions given. She handed them back.

He continued as he straightened them and put them back in the drawer. "We take photos of things people bring in and compare them to this list. Or we send the photos of the merchandise and information to the cops. Sometimes, a cop will stop in to look around and talk. As you can see, we work hand-in-hand in trying to find stolen merchandise. Not much shows up here because thieves know what we do, and they know we'll report them if something turns up."

Leona looked at her shoes. She made a mental note to

clean the dust from them when she got home. "I didn't realize."

"And as far as a black market goes, that's usually underground. You know what that means? It's all very secret, in back alleys or dives. They're not places someone like you should go poking around in. Understand? Besides, it's not really a place as much as it's an activity that's hard to pinpoint a location on. "

Leona rubbed her furrowed brow, trying to soothe the tension out of it. "Of course. I'm not a total idiot. But I'm afraid my desperation makes me look like one. I'm sorry to bother you."

The man sat back in his chair. "You seem like a nice ol—"he cleared his throat, "a nice lady. Don't let your emotions get you into trouble. There's a lot of bad people out there and I wouldn't want you going in somewhere where you might get hurt. My advice is for you to go home, go back to your knitting, and let the police handle it."

"So there's no other advice you can give me on where else to look?"

The man rolled a pencil on the desk, then rolled it back. He leaned forward across the desk and whispered, "Try the flea market. They don't always check stuff there like we do. Maybe—and I ain't promising anything—maybe they might know something. But be careful! A lot of shady characters go in them places. You could get into trouble real fast."

Leona perked up. "The flea market. The big one out on the highway? I've never been there either, but it sounds like a place I could go casually look around."

The man started to roll his eyes, but quickly rubbed them to hide it. "I don't recommend it. But if you decide to go, just watch your back. And don't announce why you're there or why you're looking. You mention stolen goods and everyone will clam up." The man leaned back. "You carry a gun?"

Leona gasped. "No! Of course not."

"You might consider it. I have some nice ones for sale. There's lots of places to learn how to use one and take care of it."

Leona shook her head and stood to go. "Thanks anyway. I'll be fine. I'll take friends with me. No one would hurt a group, right?"

The man looked doubtful. He shook his head, but offered nothing more. Leona thanked him for his time and advice and left.

7

The Christian Church Group met every Saturday morning at the best coffee house in town. No particular reason was necessary other than they liked each other's company. The shop's comfy sofas and chairs and the smell of coffee in the air provided the perfect climate in which to solve the world's problems. The conversations were always lively.

Leona carried her coffee to the sofa where the rest of the church group sat. Betty, Clarence, George, Irene, Darren, and May sat in their usual places on the chairs and sofa. Nick and Carly were still in line getting their orders so it was a little quieter and more peaceful for the time being.

"How's the clean-up coming? Are things getting back to normal?" Irene asked right before she took a bite of her bagel.

Leona and Betty sat in adjacent chairs and sipped their coffee before answering. "Slowly, but surely," Betty answered. "We got a check from the insurance so we restocked the kitchen. I'm so happy to be able to cook again. I can't do without my kitchen." She took a bite of a chocolate chip cookie she'd bought at the counter. She wrinkled her nose slightly. "Mine are better than this."

"Then don't buy them here," Leona whispered to her. She was tired of hearing the same comment every time the group met. Talking to the group, she said, "We are going shopping for living room furniture later today. I hope we'll have that in short order too. We'll be moving in on Monday, I hope. I can't wait for the new TV to get hooked up. Did I tell you we got a 60-incher?"

The group congratulated her on the purchase. Nick and Carly came and sat down. Carly's presence subdued the group somewhat so they sat in silence for a moment.

George wiped his hands on a napkin and wiped his face, cleaning off the crumbs from his second donut. He leaned back on the overstuffed leather couch and propped his large latte on his overstuffed belly. "Have the police found the thieves yet?"

Leona shook her head and told them of her frustration at the police. She told them of her visit to the pawnshop and the suggestion of the owner to get a gun. The group was appalled at the suggestion and reminded her that having a gun and Betty in the same house might be more trouble than it was worth.

"So what are you going to do?" Nick asked as he bit into his cinnamon roll.

"Go hunt for the thieves by myself," Leona said. She sat back in her chair to watch the reaction to that statement.

"Oh, you can't do that," Irene said and chuckled in disbelief. "You might get hurt! Why don't you offer a reward or something? That might get some of your stuff back."

Betty nearly spilled her coffee in excitement as she waved her arm for attention. "We could offer some of my cookies as a reward. People have told me they'd do anything to have a few of my cookies. Thieves like cookies as much as regular people." She put the last piece of cookie in her mouth, then brushed the crumbs from her lap.

The idea illuminated possibilities in Leona's mind as

well. She scolded herself for not thinking of it before. By offering as much as a pawnshop or the black market and the guarantee that no questions would be asked, maybe the thieves would return the necklace and the ring.

A huge smile spread across Leona's face that brought everyone's eyes to her. "Irene, what a fabulous idea! I'll do it! But how big of a reward do you think we should we offer?"

Betty put down her coffee cup. "I think two dozen would be plenty—no! Make it three dozen. Who could resist that?" Betty nodded her head in self-approval.

Leona frowned at Betty. "I meant money. How much money should be put up for a reward?"

Betty looked hurt. "You don't want my cookies?"

Leona patted her hand. "I'm not sure your reputation as the world's best cookie maker has reached the criminal sector yet. Let's use money. It speaks everyone's language." Giggles were muffled by hands or bites into the donuts as Betty conceded cash might be the better option.

Nick leaned forward to put his elbows on his knees. He spread his hands out. "How much you got?"

Leona calculated in her head. She had a little in savings in the bank, but that was her emergency fund. Her investments were reserved for supplementing her Social Security income. Taking care of Betty was more expensive than she'd thought it would be. She wasn't rich, only comfortable. "Not much. Maybe two hundred dollars. Do you think that's enough?"

Everyone in the group shook their head except for May. "Most rewards are more than that. Darren, we could pitch in a little, couldn't we?" Darren's eyes widened for a split second as a tinge of red spread across his face. He nodded reluctantly without looking at Leona.

"I wouldn't hear of it," Leona said after noting the change in Darren. "I don't want to owe anything to anyone. I think our best bet is to visit the flea market. We can ask some questions and see if we get anywhere. If something looks promising, I'll mention a reward."

Carly leaned forward. "I hear it's a creepy place. You might want to take some pepper spray with you. You could get attacked—"

"Where'd you hear that?" Darren brushed crumbs off his shirt. "It's just a market where people are selling things, trying to make a living. What's so creepy about that?"

Carly crossed her arms and assumed her high-brow look. "I hear things. People who've been there told me."

Nick intertwined his fingers. "Not sure what kind of people you talk to, Carly, but I think that Leona should go and find out what she can."

Betty giggled. "She can be just like Jessica Fletcher, you know, from that TV show, Murder She Wrote. You know, doing her own investigations and asking the right questions."

"Solving the mystery!" Irene raised her mug in salute.

Leona watched silently as the tittering, chuckling, and excited chatter was passed around the group. While her mission may have seemed trivial to them, she was deadly serious about finding Joe's ring. Her mother's necklace, she could let go of without much more grieving, but she wouldn't let go of Joe's ring without a fight.

"Maybe you should have taken the pawn shop man up on his offer of a gun," Betty whispered to Leona as they walked down the aisles at the flea market a few hours later. "I didn't like the looks of that man selling the sweatshirts back there." They walked closely together ahead of Clarence who stopped to look at some used books. Betty hooked her arm into Leona's arm as they crept along the crowded marketplace. With so many people pushing to look at the vendors, it was hard to stay together.

"Don't be silly, Betty! We don't need a gun. These people have businesses selling knickknacks and vegetables.

I don't see the criminal sort here. I think whoever Carly has been talking to is flat out wrong about it being creepy."

"I think it's creepy. And dirty." Betty brushed at dust gathering on her slacks. "My shoes will need a good cleaning when we get home."

"We'll look at all the booths, then go home. I'm beginning to think that man at the pawnshop sent us on a wild goose chase just to get me out of his office. I haven't seen anything shady here." She stopped to pick up a good-looking tomato. "This looks delicious!"

"It might be injected with drugs," Betty whispered loudly.

Leona closed her eyes and prayed for patience and understanding. She asked the woman behind the display for the price, then dug the money out of her purse. "I should have left you home. Where's Clarence? I thought he was right behind us."

"I think he's stuck talking to that man about his books."

"There's no room in his house for more books, although he could toss them on the pile of newspapers on the floor with the other clutter." Leona shook her head. How he could live like that, she'd never understand. Since his wife died, the once-neat home had become a cluttered mess.

Leona made her way along the dusty rows of vendors, looking for anyone who might be selling jewelry. Trinkets of every kind, t-shirts with inappropriate messages, hats of every sort, food booths, and antiques were everywhere. Most of the things, in her opinion, were just stuff. Nothing here would draw her back after they left.

One booth of antiques had a glass case and as Leona drew near, she could see jewelry inside. She shed Betty off her arm before going into the booth. Opening her purse, she pulled out the old photo of her mother wearing the necklace and showed it to the meek, spectacled, short man. "I'm looking for a necklace just like this one. It's to be a gift to my niece for her wedding. Do you have anything like it?"

The man's gruff-looking wife snatched the photo from the man's hand. Leona reached out for it, frightened that the rough woman might tear it. "I'm in charge of the jewelry. Lemme look at it." She held the photo up close to her face, then shook her head. "No, we ain't got nothing like that. We got some other pretty ones though. Your niece might like them." She waved her hand toward the glass case.

"Um, no thanks. I want a necklace very similar to this one for sentimental reasons." Leona got her photo back and quickly tucked it away in her purse. "Do you have any gold bands for men that you have recently purchased?"

The lady shook her head. "Not since last month." She pounded her large index finger on the glass case. "Look over what we got. There's some nice ones here."

Leona glanced over the selection. Most of them seemed rather new, not worn like Joe's ring. She mentioned this to the lady.

"Our customers want new-looking rings. The old ones, well, nobody wants 'em so we sell them to the gold people. They melt 'em down and get like the gold and silver and stuff outta them."

Leona gasped and clutched at her heart. Hearing those words again struck her in the heart. Her last remaining tie with Joe may be in some golden blob in a back room somewhere. Desperation and heartache almost forced a cry of anguish out of her, but she swallowed it back down. She dug through her purse looking for a tissue. Finding one, she wiped her nose.

The woman stared at her with worried eyes. Leona waved her concerns off. "I'm fine. Just a quick spell. Thanks for your help." She turned to go and nearly ran into Betty who was right behind her. Her eyes were smiling as she grabbed her sister's arm and lead her away.

"Come with me," Betty whispered to her sister. She went quickly, weaving in and out between people past a furniture vendor and another antique dealer. Betty kept tugging on Leona until they reached a jewelry vendor at the end of an aisle. Betty excitedly pointed to several wood-and-glass display cases full of costume and gemstone jewelry. "Maybe it's here," Betty whispered.

The sisters held on to each other as they walked slowly along each glass case, carefully looking at the variety of gold wedding bands and necklaces, some of which looked old, but none looked like Joe's plain band. Leona's heart fell. "It's not here."

A man with a Cowboys t-shirt that barely covered his bulbous belly came up to the ladies. The tattoos on his arms ran all the way up and under his sleeves. "Sumpin you wanna see?" He cocked his hip and Leona wondered if just the one leg could hold up all that weight.

"We're just looking for now," she said as she stared at the tattoo on his neck, trying to figure out what it depicted. Giving up, she and Betty turned back to the large wooden case covered with glass to look among the many necklaces inside. Tattoo Man eyed them, but left them to their perusing. He walked back to his seat at the rear of his booth and kept a close eye on them.

Leona searched through several dozen men's wedding bands, hoping against hope that she'd see Joe's ring. As with the previous booth, most of the rings here looked new or only slightly used. Disappointed again, she stepped back from the case. "At least there are gold bands around. I guess we keep looking." She turned to leave the booth.

Betty grabbed her sister's arm and pulled her back. "No, no, no. That's not what I wanted you to look at. Come look over here, in the back." Betty led her to another glass case filled with necklaces of every description. She pointed to a blue bead necklace near the back of the case. "Isn't that the necklace I gave you for Christmas one year? Yours had an odd clasp and see here? This blue bead necklace has the same odd clasp. In fact, I think this one is yours!"

Leona followed where she was pointing and gasped. If it wasn't hers, it was an exact replica of it. Her heart skipped a beat as she frantically searched through the other necklaces. Her mother's was nowhere to be seen. She waved at Tattoo Man who was feasting on what appeared to be a large mound of chili-covered French fries. He licked his fingers and wiped them dry on his shirt before he got up.

"Ya need something?" He let out a soft belch.

Leona tried hard not to wrinkle her nose or close her eyes in disgust. "Yes, please. That blue bead necklace in the back. Can I see that?"

Tattoo Man pulled a full ring of keys from his pocket and fumbled through half of them before finding the one that would unlock the case. With great ceremony, he pulled the necklace out and laid it on top of the case. Leona and Betty leaned over it for a closer view. After seeing the man lick his fingers, neither of them wanted to pick it up. Leona pushed the beads around with her fingernail. The urge to shower swept over her like a flash flood, but she went to higher philosophical ground.

"This looks just like a necklace I used to have," she said, looking up at Tattoo Man. "How much is it?" She looked at the tiny tag, then dug in her purse to start looking for her magnifying glass.

Tattoo Man picked it up and said, "Tag says it's $10. Nice piece of costume jewelry. It would look good on you."

Betty offered, "That's what I said when I bought it for you." Tattoo Man frowned.

Leona punched her sister to hush. "I'm curious. Do you know where it came from? Where you got it?"

"Not really. I think my uncle got it from an estate sale somewhere. Why?"

She shrugged. "No reason." She pulled the photo of her mother out of her purse. "Do you have a necklace that looks like this? I want one for my niece."

The man looked at it for a long time. "I'm not sure. Seems familiar." He looked through the jewelry in the case for a few minutes. "Hang here while I check the back." He put the blue bead necklace back in the case and locked it again before leaving.

"That's my blue necklace!" Leona said when he was out of earshot. "I'm sure of it. Maybe he has Joe's ring and Mother's necklace in the back. If they're not, all I have to do is find out where he got it. That will give us a new lead to follow." Her throat emitted a cackle that startled both ladies. Leona was afraid she was starting to lose control of herself.

"Are you going to make him give you your blue necklace back?"

"No, I'll buy them off him so he doesn't know we're suspicious, but I'll pressure him about it if I have to. I want to know where he got it or from whom. I want Joe's ring back and I'll do whatever it takes to get it." Leona tapped out an impatient rhythm with her fingernails on the top of the glass case. "Oh Lord, please let my things be back there."

Betty uttered an "Amen."

After a few minutes, the man came back and said he couldn't find it. "I guess I's wrong about it. We don't got one like that. Everything we got is in the cases. Wanna look at anything else?"

"If I knew where your uncle got this blue necklace, I could contact that person to see if he or she had more jewelry. Could you find out where he got this? It's exactly what I'm looking for."

Tattoo Man stepped back, suddenly unsure of her intentions. "He may not remember. He buys stuff from all kinds of people. People're always looking to sell stuff. You gonna buy the blue one or not?"

"I'll buy it, if you tell me who he bought it from. In fact, I'll pay you $20 for it, if you give me that information."

Shuffling his feet, Tattoo Man narrowed his eyes and looked out the side of them. "Why you gotta know that?"

"Because this is MY necklace that was stolen from me last week. And I want the thug who stole it from me!" Leona stopped, horrified at herself for using her bad-day teacher's voice. The floodgates of aggravation had opened and rushed out all at once before she could stop it. *Oh well, let it flow,* she told herself. She let the anger continue to spill. "Do you hear me? I want my mother's necklace back. The one in the picture! It was in the same box as the blue necklace."

A crowd gathered around the booth, watching as Leona's voice grew louder. They whispered to each other, staring as the elderly woman gripped the jewelry case. Was she going to tip it over? Would she break the glass? The murmurs suggested that she would do something to give them a show.

Betty quietly tugged at Leona's arm to pull her back a little. Seeing the fear in the large man's eyes and feeling the tugging, Leona regained her composure. She lowered her voice enough so the large man could hear her, but no one else could. "You can keep everything the thief took from me, except for the necklace in the photo and my husband's gold wedding band. Give them to me and tell me where you got them. In return, I won't tell the police about you. If you don't tell me what I want to know, I'll call the police about you dealing in stolen goods. And don't think I won't!" Leona shook her finger at him to emphasize her impatience. She waited for a response. Getting none, she continued. "What's it going to be?" Leona set her jaw.

Beads of sweat broke out on Tattoo Man's upper lip. He looked nervously around at the crowd just outside his booth. "Keep your voice down. You're running off my customers." He looked around sheepishly at the gathered crowd and smiled. "Come on in and look around, folks. Nothing going on here but dealing." He waved his arms to welcome people in, but got no takers.

He leaned across the counter and looked Leona square in the eye. "We don't take stolen goods if we know they're stolen. If anything here is stolen, whoever sold it to my uncle fooled him into thinking he owned it. Maybe that necklace in the picture looked sorta like another one. I got mixed up. I don't know. They all look alike to me." He unlocked the case, pulled the blue bead necklace out, and flung it at her. She caught it as it started sliding down the front of her blouse. "That your necklace? Take it. You see your husband's wedding band? Take it. Whatever is yours, take it. Then get outta here!"

Leona quickly put the blue necklace in her purse and zipped it shut. Leona stared at his face. She sensed nervousness, like a sidekick left holding the bag and a guilty look. "First, tell me who gave these to your uncle."

Tattoo Man's knuckles whitened as he gripped the edge of the glass case. The sweat on his upper lip had spread to his forehead. He leaned across the counter and whispered, "No. It's not good for business, if I tell who brings stuff to me and my uncle."

"The police will be bad for your business too. So you can either tell me or tell them. You pick."

Tattoo Man tapped his fingers on the glass case as he held a debate with himself about what to do. He heaved a heavy sigh and said, "I think his name is T-bone. He comes from the north end of town, up around Seventh Street. That's all I know! I've told you more than I should. Now go and leave me the—"

Betty interrupted the man. "Don't say it! Thou shalt not take the Lord's name in vain!" She wagged her finger at the man. "By thy words thou shalt be justified and—"

"Enough!" He bellowed and waved them off. "Git! And never come back!"

Betty backed away and left, but turned around to come back to drag Leona away from her stare-down contest with

Tattoo Man. She pulled her sister along as quickly as her legs could carry her. They rushed past Clarence who yelled after them to slow down.

Leona had the minivan started when Clarence finally got there, squeaking and puffing like an old stream engine. Betty filled him in on what happened as she helped him into the minivan.

"No!" Clarence yelled at Leona as Betty put his walker in the back of the minivan. "We're not going on the north side. That's the bad part of town!"

Leona looked over her shoulder at him. "I didn't say anything about that."

"I know you. That's where you intend to go. Call the police and let them take care of it. Who was that detective guy? Call him. You've done enough investigating on your own."

"I'm only just beginning," said Leona as she drove away.

8

On the way out of the large parking lot, Clarence made it quite clear that he objected to going to the north side of town. "Good people don't go there," he'd said. When Leona refused to give in, he whined that he felt like a hostage being transported to places he didn't want to go. The silent treatment ended the argument as they headed north. Clarence sat in the backseat with narrowed eyes and pursed lips that told the story of his mood. Betty looked out her side of the minivan at the passing landscape, not saying a word. Leona didn't want to hear a word out of either of them.

Leona was thinking about what to do if she found this T-bone character. She'd never confronted a thug before—at least, she assumed that was what he probably was. Having never confronted a thug, she wasn't sure she knew how to do it. How would she defend herself if he attacked? He might if he knew she suspected him in burglarizing her home. But was he the burglar? How would she find out for sure? Somehow, she had to stay cool and calm. And sensible. She couldn't let him know how she found out his name. As much as she didn't like Tattoo Man, she didn't wish him any harm.

She gripped the steering wheel even harder as the thoughts roiled through her mind. She needed a plan. That's what Joe always said: have a plan. But how could she plan for something she had never experienced? There were too many variables and likely more variables that she'd never think of on her own.

As she turned the minivan down Seventh Street, dread filled her. She had rarely been to this side of town. Joe had always told her to stay away. He said ninety percent of all crime in town was in this area. What would he say to her now, driving down this street in the late afternoon on a Saturday? He would be furious with her.

This neighborhood stood in stark contrast to her older, well-established neighborhood. The houses here were old, from another era. Almost all were ill-kept and badly in need of repairs. The yards were either covered in dirt or the weeds were knee-deep so that it looked like a jungle. Rusted cars and bits and pieces of toys lay beside the houses or in the yards. The trash-strewn gutters and neighborhood screamed out in neglect.

The visible poverty of the surroundings ended the silent treatment pact in the minivan. Betty broke the silence first. "What kind of people name their son after meat? Seems like a silly name to me."

"It's probably a nickname," Leona said as she weaved around the potholes that riddled the street while keeping an eye out for people. So far, they'd seen no one. The neighborhood and streets seemed to be deserted.

"This is a bad idea!" Clarence repeated from the backseat. "And don't even think of shushing me. Joe would agree with me. You should call Smythe and tell him about this T-bone character."

"I will after we find him." Leona slowed a little when they met the first car they'd seen since they turned down this street.

Clarence let out a grunt of disapproval. "What are we

going to do when we find him? Walk up and say, 'Did you burglarize my house?" Can I get my stuff back from you?'"

"I won't accuse him of anything. I'm just going to ask him to give back the ring and necklace," Leona said, trying not to shout it out. She gritted her teeth to keep from saying anything she'd regret. She took a deep breath to calm the last of her frazzled nerves. "That's it. That's all I'm going to do. I even brought $20 to give him for his trouble."

"And I brought cookies," Betty offered. She picked up her huge bag and pulled out a small tin. "Chocolate chip. No one can resist chocolate chip cookies."

Clarence grunted again. "That's not much money. You should offer more. I thought you were going to pay $200."

"I didn't get by the bank. It's all I have with me."

Clarence grumbled like a lion. "And how are you going to find him? Start knocking on doors? How do you know he'll even tell you who he is? And how do you know that he'll even talk to you?"

"Tempt him with my cookies first." Betty smiled with pride and shook the tin slightly, as if it would add weight to the trade.

"I'm sure he'll do anything for cookies," Clarence said, his voice dripping with sarcasm. "I still say call Smythe first and then ask questions later. Let him do his job and we'll stay out of his way. We're out of our league!"

Leona shook her head but inside, she knew he was right. They had nothing with which to defend themselves in this hostile territory. The thought of the pawnshop owner telling her she needed a gun kept returning. Deep in her heart, she wasn't sure she could use it to hurt someone else. And if she couldn't, then there wasn't much use of having one.

She turned a corner and saw a group of teenagers standing on the sidewalk. Some of them ignored the minivan driving by while others stared so intently that it made the hair on the back of her neck stand on end. Maybe having a gun wasn't such a bad idea. She decided she'd think more of it later.

A shot of adrenaline flashed through her heart, making it flutter. *What am I thinking? I would never use a gun, especially on children or teenagers. I must be losing my mind to even think it! Lord, please forgive me and help me through this.*

Up ahead, Leona saw three people standing on the steps of a dilapidated house. The screen material on the door was hanging down and the front window had cardboard where glass used to be. An expensive, newer car sat beside the house, looking completely out of place. The people looked young, maybe in their twenties and the two young men and a young woman were talking lightheartedly, punching each other on the arms, laughing, and passing around a brown paper bag. There didn't seem to be anything to worry about. Just friends hanging out. One of the young men put his arm around the woman and pulled her close.

"Maybe they know T-bone," Leona said as she slowed the minivan. She pulled to the curb on the opposite side of the street and stopped. The maneuver interrupted the young people's conversation and they all looked at the vehicle. They stared as Leona rolled her window down. "Excuse me, can you help me?"

They looked at each other. The tall skinny young man sauntered over toward the minivan. He stopped about twenty feet away and put his hands into the pockets of his faded hoodie. His clothes, especially his pants, looked like they were made for a giant of a man. Leona had seen this kind of garb on TV and had often wondered how the boys managed to keep their pants on without them falling around their feet. She fought the urge to get out of the minivan to go pull up his baggy pants.

The young man looked at the old folks with a slight smile and a slight waver to his stance. The other young man and the girl came up behind him. The few clothes the girl had on were very tight, outlining her slim body. The young man with his arm around her waist looked like he fell off a GQ magazine cover. Judging from his clothes, the car must have been his.

Baggy Pants spoke. "You lost? The old folks home is back the other way." He grinned and turned to share his sarcasm with his companions. They joined in with his laughter.

Leona gritted her teeth, then relaxed her jaw. Forcing what she hoped was a warm smile, she said, "We're looking for someone named T-bone. Have you ever heard of him?"

The people looked at each other and snickered. "Why you lookin' for him?"

Clarence yelled from the backseat, "Oh, then you do know him. We just want to ask him a couple of questions, that's all. Then we'll be on our way. We don't want to cause trouble."

Baggy Pants leaned down and looked inside the minivan at Clarence. "I don't know y'all or why y'all'er here. You need to turn this bus around and go on home before trouble finds you."

Betty leaned over, "Do you like cookies?" She held out her tin and rattled it a little. Pulling the lid off, she showed them her neat little stacks of sugary delights. She passed them to Leona who held the tin out the window.

Baggy Pants walked up and leaned against the car, with the couple not far behind him. He eyed the offered tin suspiciously. "Sumpin wrong with those cookies?"

Betty looked surprised. "Why no! They're delicious! I make the best cookies in Texas. Or maybe the world!"

The man gingerly took the tin and pulled it outside. He took a cookie and bit a small piece off. A sugar-powered smile spread over his face as he held out the tin to his two companions and waved at them. They each took a cookie to taste. Smiles spread across their faces as they took several more of them. Baggy Pants quickly stuffed another cookie into his mouth.

Betty smirked at Leona and Clarence. "I knew you'd like them! So can you tell us where T-bone lives? We need to ask him about some things that were taken from our house."

Leona quickly shushed Betty. "We weren't going to say anything about that," she whispered. Turning back to the window, she watched the young people eating and laughing with each other about something she didn't understand. When they started walking away, she leaned out the window and called after them, "You didn't tell us where to find a man named T-bone."

"Why you need to fin' him?" Baggy Pants asked with his cheeks stuffed with cookies. He stuffed his mouth with the last of the cookies and threw the tin into the yard.

Betty started to get out, but Clarence grabbed her arm and told her to stay inside the minivan. Leona locked the car doors and hoped the three young people hadn't heard the deafening click. She squeezed the steering wheel with an iron grip, resisting the urge to speed away.

Leona watched as Baggy Pants put his hands in his hoodie pockets. Visions of guns flashed across her mind, causing her heart to beat even faster. She held her hands out the window so they could see she was unarmed. *Get this over with*, she told herself. "We just want to ask a few questions. That's all. Then we'll leave and you won't see us again."

"Never heard of him," the young woman yelled at them. "Go home. You don't belong around here."

"Yes, we should go," Clarence urged in a loud whisper.

"I want my cookie tin back," Betty whispered loudly.

"I'll buy you a new one," he replied as he held her arm. "Stay in the car!"

Leona's last frazzled nerve gave way. "Please!" she shouted. "I'm looking for my mother's necklace and my late husband's wedding ring that was stolen from our house. That's all I want. Nothing else. No questions. No police. Please!"

Baggy Pants stopped and turned to face the minivan. Well-dressed Man came up beside him and stood in a wide stance with crossed arms. An evil grin came across the face of Baggy Pants. He lifted his hand in a gesture that made Leona's face redden.

Leona let her foot relax on the brake and the minivan started to slowly move away. "Thanks anyway," she yelled as they drove away. The trio in the minivan watched the young people as they pointed and laughed at the oldsters leaving the scene.

Leona went to the end of the block and turned the corner to get out of sight of the rude behavior. "That went well," she said sarcastically. "They thought we were idiots. And they're right."

Betty gasped and slapped her knee. "We forgot about the reward money. Maybe you should have offered them the $20 for information."

Clarence shouted an emphatic "NO!" so loudly that it choked him. After his spate of coughing, he said hoarsely, "They'd have wanted more. And they might have robbed us. Don't bring money into the offer unless you want to lose that too."

A sigh of resignation escaped Leona's lips. She was at a dead end in her investigation. How was she going to find this T-bone character in a neighborhood like this? Clarence was probably right. The offer of money would have made the situation worse. Moreover, what would she have done if one of them had been T-bone? She shook her head very slightly. All she wanted was Joe's ring. And her mother's necklace, but that didn't really matter all that much anymore. Joe's ring. Her heart ached to have it back again. To see it on his pillow once again. So she could feel he was close by once again.

Clarence was right about something else. It was time to go to Smythe and tell him what she'd found out. Maybe this information would spur him to action.

She guided the minivan along the street, crawling at a snail's pace, checking her rearview mirror to make sure they were not being followed by Baggy Pants and Suit Guy.

Betty pointed ahead. "What about asking those boys? They don't look nearly as intimidating as that last group who threw away my cookie tin."

Leona followed Betty's pointing finger to see a group of three boys, stair-stepped in age with the oldest looking to be about eight or nine years old. The oldest boy was herding the other two down the street. Their dark, unkempt hair matched their faded ill-fitting clothes. The two oldest boys wore shoes, but the youngest one didn't.

"You should have saved your cookies for them," Clarence told Betty.

Betty reached under the seat and brought out another small tin. "I always carry spares." She let out a chuckle of triumph as she pried the lid off the tin.

Leona pulled the minivan to the curb beside the boys and stopped. The oldest boy protectively pulled the other two toward the nearest yard. Large brown eyes watched Betty as she rolled her window down.

"Don't be afraid," Betty said in a soft grandmotherly voice. "We just want to ask you a question. And I have cookies, if you'd like some." She held the small tin out the window.

The oldest boy stood on his toes to look inside the tin, but he stayed away from the minivan. He licked his lips as he held on tight to the younger boys.

"We are looking for someone named T-bone. You ever heard of him?"

The youngest boy's face brightened. "T-bone! I like…" The oldest boy put his hand over the young boy's mouth and told him to shut up.

"We don't know nobody named T-bone. Why you wanna know?" The older boy let go of the boy's mouth and gently pushed him along in front of him as they continued down the street.

"No cookies then." Betty pulled the tin back inside. The youngest boy let out a moan of disappointment. The oldest boy pushed him along. Leona put the minivan in reverse and crept along with the boys.

The boys stopped and stood in the dirt-covered yard. The littlest one looked up at the tallest one. "I'm hungry. I want some cookies."

Before the oldest boy could say yes or no, the middle boy ran to the minivan with his hand out. Betty kept the tin inside the vehicle out of reach. "You didn't answer my question. Do you know someone named T-bone?"

The boy nodded and Betty handed him a cookie which he bit into eagerly. The youngest boy ran over and said, "I know him too!" Betty handed him a cookie. He stuffed it in his mouth and reached for another. Betty gave him one.

The eldest boy came over and held his hand out. Betty filled it with a cookie. "Can you tell us where we can find him?"

The boys stood with outreached hands and cookie-filled mouths, unable to talk coherently. The sight made Leona smile, but she felt a twinge of guilt for feeding hungry boys empty calories instead of something nutritious. *Oh well*, she thought, *a little sugar won't hurt them that much.*

Clarence opened his door of the minivan. The boys watched wide-eyed as the automatic door open itself. "Hello! What's your names?"

The oldest boy took a big swallow. "I'm Doran. This here's my brother, Jaden and the little boy is my cousin, Tiger. What's your name?"

"Nice to meet you, Doran. I'm Clarence. The cookie lady is Betty and our chauffeur is Leona." The ladies waved and smiled at the boys as they continued eating.

Betty rattled the remaining cookies in the tin. "Just a few left. You can have them, if you answer one question. Do you know where we can find T-bone?"

"Right here." A deep voice came from behind the minivan. Leona looked in the rearview mirror and saw Baggy Pants and Suit Man from around the corner, along with a very large man who looked even less friendly than the other two. The three of them had their tattooed arms crossed and stood with their feet wide apart, ready for a fight.

9

Doran gathered the other two boys in his arms and pulled them away from the minivan. Baggy Pants ran and grabbed the boys, slapping at them as he tried to hold them. Some must have landed because the sound of punches filled the air. Doran cried out in pain. The man threw Doran to the ground and tried to kick him.

Clarence got out, hanging onto the minivan for support. "You stop that! Don't you hurt those boys!" Without his walker, he couldn't go any farther. "Leave them alone!" he yelled as loudly as he could.

"Run!" Doran screamed out as he rolled away from the kicking feet of Baggy Pants. The young boys took off, with Suit Man and the big guy close behind them.

Unable to believe her eyes, Leona sat in the minivan in stunned silence. Doran's scream shocked her out of her stupor, and she got out of the minivan shouting, "Those boys didn't say anything. Leave them alone." She ran toward Doran and pushed Baggy Pants away while she helped Doran out of the dirt. She pointed him toward the minivan where Betty had the door open and was waving for him to come. Leona backed up toward the minivan.

"We were trying to find T-bone because we wanted to

talk to him about some things taken from our house." The big man came up holding the two smallest boys off the ground by their arms. He threw them on the ground at Leona's feet.

Suit Man had a scowl on his face. "You callin' me a thief? You gotta lot of nerve, lady!" He squared off at her. His fists were clenched and he stood ready to move. The two smallest boys stayed huddled next to Leona, with eyes as big as saucers. She directed them behind her and heard Betty call them to her.

Leona's heart was beating so loudly she could hardly hear herself think as she stared at Suit Guy. "Then I assume you're T-bone. Look, I'm not calling you a thief. Someone—I don't know who—robbed our house and took some things that are very sentimental to me. We got a tip that you might know what happened to them. I just want to know if you can help me find my very special ring and necklace. That's all I want to know."

"A tip? Someone gave you a tip that I might have your junk? Who's the rat?" He shoved Leona and she stumbled backwards. In an unacrobatic move, she managed to keep her balance, but it left her head spinning. She stumbled toward the front bumper of the minivan to catch her balance and stop her dizziness.

"Look, all I want to know is…" She took a deep breath and it seemed to clear her head. She stepped away from the minivan and back into the yard near the sidewalk. "…can you help me find my husband's wedding band?" Her voice broke as she struggled with the tension. "He died two years ago and it's all I have left of him. I desperately want it back. The thief can have everything else. I just want my husband's ring. Please. Have a heart!"

"What's goin' on here?" A woman's voice rang out over the yard. "What ch'all doin' in my yard?"

"Nothin'," T-bone called out over his shoulder. "Go back in your house, Miz Molly."

"Is that you, Terrance?" A large woman came up behind him and stared at Leona and the others. Tall and stout, she looked as powerful and as threatening as an elephant matriarch defending her family. Her faded floral muumuu and flipflops added to her aura as queen of the jungle.

"Don't call me that!" T-bone hissed at her. "Now git back in your house. I and Jay is talking with these people."

In the distance, a siren was dimly heard. Leona saw fright flash in T-bone's eyes before it was replaced by anger. T-bone took a step toward her. She stepped back and held her hands up. "I'm just an old lady trying to find my husband's ring!"

"That's the truth!" Betty got out of the car and pushed past the little boys. "Don't you hurt my sister!" She ran toward T-bone. Baggy Pants agilely stepped around the others and pushed Betty backward so hard that she fell. She lay motionless.

"Betty!" Leona screamed as she rushed toward her inert sister. T-bone pushed her down beside Betty. He then grabbed the front of her blouse and pulled her up close to his face.

"Get outta my hood!" Leona hit at his hands trying to break free.

Clarence wobbled his way toward the prostrate women. He was barely standing and was no threat to them. "I'm a Korean war veteran! I'm not afraid to fight!" He teetered as he held his fists up.

Leona looked up at the three men, unsure of what to do next. The large woman came up to T-bone and mocked him. "Such a big man, Terrance. Pushing around kids and old people! You're all bullies!" She pointed to Betty who lay still on the ground. "If you've hurt her, I'll press charges and then the police will come looking for you."

The large woman grabbed the collars of Baggy Pants and the large man and took them around to the other side of the minivan. "You're not allowed on my side of the street! Go back to your side. And don't cross it again!" She shoved them and they stumbled a few steps before regaining their swaggers.

T-bone came up beside Leona. For an instant, she thought he was going to hit her. He opened his mouth to say something, but he restrained his tongue. He straightened his collar and strutted across the street behind his boys. They all stopped when they reached the curb on the other side.

T-bone swirled around and pointed at Miz Molly. "You keep those old fogies on your side of the street. And you, old lady..." He pointed at Leona. "Don't ever come around accusing me of being a thief. I won't be so kind to you next time!" With a flurry of foul language and rude gestures, the three men trotted off down the street before disappearing into an alleyway.

Leona rolled over and checked Betty for a pulse. A soft thumping gave the answer she was hoping for. Betty moaned a little when Leona patted her cheek. "Betty, dear, can you open your eyes? Betty, please say something."

The large woman leaned over Betty and looked at her. "Is she dead?" The boys joined her in looking down on the prostrate women.

"No, I'm not dead," Betty said, opening one eye and fighting an unbidden smile. "Scared you, didn't I?" She giggled. "I figured if they thought I was dead, they'd leave us alone. Must have worked."

Leona sat up and let out an exasperated sigh of relief. "Betty! You scared the daylights out of me. I thought for sure they'd broken your hip or worse."

The large woman knelt down beside Betty. "You're lucky it's not. Looked like you landed hard."

"I'll certainly have a bruise, but no bones seem to be broken. All those years of drinking milk from Papa's cows have paid off." Betty rolled over and tried to sit up.

"I think I scared them off," Clarence called out from beside the minivan. "I must've looked pretty formidable to them." He laughed at himself as he inched his way back to his seat before he fell down.

Leona slowly got up off the ground with the aid of the boys. The large woman helped pull her to her feet. Betty tittered and held her arms out for help. The boys took her arms and with much grunting and moaning, they managed to sit her up. The boys, the large woman, and Leona managed to get Betty up and help her stumble her way to the minivan.

Leona looked at the boys and could see bruises starting to form where the men had hit them. She let out a cry of alarm and pulled them to her. Doran had a little blood coming from his nose and the smallest was rubbing his leg. "Are you hurt? Betty, hand me one of those tissues."

"Naw, we're used to it." Doran wiped his nose on the tissue offered by Betty.

Betty cried out. "Used to it? No child should get used to that kind of treatment! It's abuse!"

Doran shook his head without saying anything. Tiger smiled and asked, "Can we have some more cookies?"

Betty handed the tin to the boys. "You've earned them!"

The large woman leaned against the minivan. "Who are you? What are you doing on this side of town? If I hadn't heard the boys yelling, you could have been badly hurt. Terrance and his gang are no people to fool around with."

"I'm Leona Templeton and the cookie lady is my sister, Betty Drummond. Our manly escort is Clarence Brown." Leona wiped her dusty hand on her slacks and held it out in friendship. "Thank you for coming to our rescue."

The large woman raised an eyebrow, then took her hand and shook it. "They call me Miz Molly."

Miz Molly pointed to the boys and said, "I guess you already know Doran, the protector..." She pointed to the middle boy, "...Jaden, the one who gets into trouble all the time..." Jaden gave a squinty smile as he stuffed another cookie into his mouth. "...and Tiger, the quiet one who watches everything you do." She gave a big smile. "Considering where these boys come from, they're real nice kids."

Betty gave the boys the last cookies in the tin. "Are you their mother?"

Miz Molly put her finger across her lips. "Boys, why don't you go inside and watch TV. Kendra and Zilo are in there and you can play with them a while." The boys ran off, going into the next-door ramshackle house with a bang of the screenless screen door.

Clarence let out a grumpy sound. "They didn't even say thanks for the cookies."

Betty frowned. "Hush, Clarence! You didn't tell them thank you either." She turned back to Miz Molly and asked, "Where do they come from?"

Miz Molly shook her head. "A bad place. Their mom is drunk most of the time and she sells herself for extra money. How those boys have stayed sweet souls, I'll never understand. They need a good home, but I can't give it. I'm raising my grandkids and I ain't got room for more."

A lump was making its presence known in Leona's throat and her eyes were getting misty. She could tell they were good boys. "Is there anything we can do to help?"

Miz Molly's eyebrows shot up, then they came back down as she shook her head. "Get 'em a new home I guess. But enough of that. Y'all need to go home and not come back to this side of town. Why did you come here in the first place? You don't belong here."

Betty waved her hand to get everyone's attention. "You won't believe our story. It started the day Al Watson saved our lives."

"I told you to stay out of it!" Detective Smythe said it loudly enough so that everyone in the police station lobby looked over at them. "We—not you—are investigating. You're going to mess it up if you don't quit poking your noses into things you don't know anything about." He paced around the reception area, running his hand through his hair in frustration. "And who are these kids? Why are they here?"

"They're our witnesses," Leona said. She stood beside the bench where Doran, Jaden, and Tiger sat, all dressed in new clothes purchased just that morning. "We thought you might want to ask them questions."

Betty, also sitting on the bench, put her arms around the three boys. "We offered to take them to McDonalds if they helped us out. You agreed, right, boys?"

Big smiles spread across the boys' faces as they nodded.

"So you bribed them to say whatever you told them to say." Detective Smythe glared at her and continued pacing. "Do the parents of these kids know they've been kidnapped and taken to the police station? The lure of food is one of the ruses child molesters use to take kids."

The elderly trio all gasped and talked at the same time, denying such an intention. The boys fidgeted and watched the adults arguing.

Detective Smythe gave a one-sided smile. "I know, but technically, I could make a case against you."

"We didn't kidnap them! They came willingly," Leona said louder than she had intended. "And not because we have any evil intent. On the contrary, we'd like to help these boys as much as we can." She took a moment to calm herself. "Look, we found some valuable information for you. You should be thanking us. We found out that T-bone's gang lives in that house on 7th Street. Why can't you raid it? I bet there's all kinds of loot in there."

He pinched the bridge of his nose as he made a face behind his hand. "No, you got nothing but hearsay from some kids you found on the street and promised food to in exchange for them telling the story you told them to tell.

That's not enough for a warrant. All you've done is let him know that we're on his trail. You've spooked him and he'll be careful now. He'll back out of his activities for a while, until things settle down. You've managed to stretch this investigation out longer."

The trio sat in silence on the benches as the boys squirmed beside them. Her good intentions had turned into bad ideas. Leona could feel the necklace and the ring slipping away for good. She put her hand to her trembling chin to keep it from pushing too many tears out.

Tiger got off the bench and came over to Leona. He looked up at her with his large pleading eyes. "Can we go to McDonalds now?"

Smythe gave them one last hateful look before starting toward his office in the back. "I have to get back to work and somehow try to salvage the damage you've caused." He went out of the room without another word.

Betty smiled at the boys who were staring at her and wondering about how soon they'd get to McDonalds. Leona stood staring at the floor. Clarence pushed his walker back and forth in impatience to go. The wheel squeaked like an alarm saying it was time to leave.

Leona's heart was in her stomach and her shoulders felt very heavy. She'd made things worse with her wild ideas of investigating on her own. She couldn't remember why it had seemed a good idea to bring the boys to the police station. Last night in the dark, it had seemed like one. Now she'd have Carly asking why they weren't at church that morning.

Betty was the first to move down the hall. The boys followed close on her heels. Clarence stood up and pushed his walker, squeaking along behind them. With herculean effort, Leona lifted her heavy burden and followed the others outside.

10

Leona slowed the minivan in front of a house that looked like it should be condemned. It looked more like a shed than a house. The yard was rocks and weeds surrounded by a broken wooden fence that had once been painted white. The weeds growing around a rusty old car told the story of how long it had been parked there. The uneven sidewalk went to a deteriorating concrete step. The screen door hung at an angle in front of the faded entry door.

Leona turned off the engine and said, "This is where you live?" She pushed the buttons to open the minivan's rear door and side door. The boys clamored out and went to the back of the minivan where several bags of groceries sat. They took the bags and with an excited clamor, went up the crumbling walkway. Leona followed quietly behind. The boys disappeared into the house, leaving Leona on the front step.

"Yoo hoo!" She peeked inside the door that was ajar. "I need to talk to the boys' mother to explain where they were."

The door swung open and startled Leona. A skinny boy, looking to be about 12 or 13, stood there with a cigarette hanging from his lips. "You the one that gave them boys some food?"

"Why, yes," she said. "It's in return for a favor they did for us earlier today. Is their mother around?"

The young man turned back to the living room, calling back over his shoulder. "She's doing yard work out back."

Leona gingerly stepped inside the room. It was tiny and filthy, with a worn and tattered sofa and one folding chair filling the room. The boy plopped on the sofa to watch a blaring big screen TV sitting on a folding table, spewing obscenities and sexual innuendoes. Leona was horrified by the noise and put her fingers in her ears. Doran came back and said, "Mom can't see you now. Maybe some other day."

"Are you sure? I think it best that I explain things to her."

Jaden called from the back door. "I'll take you to see her." Doran protested again, but Leona pushed past him. She went through a kitchen where dishes covered the table and countertops, looking like they'd been there for years. The groceries they'd bought for the boys were piled on top of the mess on the table. Likely nothing would ever be put away in the dirty cabinets which was probably for the best. It would be more sanitary if they were used straight from the sack.

She went out the back door into a grassy area that looked like a hay pasture. To one side, a woman lay face up with her eyes closed. A line of drool ran from her mouth down the side of her head. Leona bent over to make sure she was still breathing. She was.

Leona stood and looked at Jaden. "I thought that young man said she was doing yard work?"

"That's what we call it when she's passed out."

"Is she like this often?"

"Not all the time, but a lot."

Leona shook her head. "No child should ever see this."

She straightened up and put her arm around the boy's shoulders and took him back into the house.

"Okay, well, I guess I'll leave now." She turned to go. "Thank you for your help today. I hope you and your brothers will be okay."

"Thanks for the food. Would you take us to McDonalds again sometime?" He followed her to the door.

Leona stepped outside. "Maybe. Someday. We may drop off more food from time to time as well."

"I'd like that!" He flashed a huge grin. The boys stood in line to get their hugs, eager for them.

When Leona got back in the minivan, Betty and Clarence asked her about what she saw. Leona could hardly speak it, the scene had so repulsed her. She shook her head at their questions and blinked away the tears as she drove home.

The ladies checked out of the hotel the next morning. The house was ready again and none too soon. Both of the ladies were anxious to get back to their familiar surroundings.

Leona left Betty and Clarence having coffee at the house while she went back to the police station. She had an unsettled feeling in the pit of her stomach that had kept her up all night. She had to settle the matter without further delay.

The desk sergeant was in his usual foul mood, refusing to let her see Detective Smythe. She calmly sat on a bench, took out her cell phone, and called the number on Smythe's business card. He answered quickly.

"Detective Smythe, where are you?" Leona asked, sweet as sugar.

"I'm at work. Who is this?" Even with not knowing it was her, his tone of voice was irritated.

"This is Leona Templeton. I need to talk to you and the sergeant out here won't let me in. Can you tell him you're working on my burglary case so he'll let me come in and talk with you?"

The man didn't answer for a moment. "What do you want, Leona." It wasn't a question.

His demanding tone didn't surprise her. She knew he disliked her as much as she disliked him, but at this point, he was her only option. She said, "There is a new matter that I need to discuss with you. It won't take more than a few moments."

A heavy sigh came through the phone. "Two minutes tops." He hung up without saying another word. The next instant, the front desk phone rang and the sergeant growled that Leona could go back. She tried hard not to smirk, although a slight one leaked out.

The detective was leaning against the wall in the hallway with his arms crossed. "What's so important?" he called out as she made her way past several police officers. "I'm too busy to put up with more of your meddling."

Leona frowned at the man who was not her idea of a good public servant. "I want to talk to you about those boys that we brought here yesterday."

He stood up and uncrossed his arms. "What about them?"

"I told you about those thugs threatening the boys. I'm worried about them. Can you send someone out to check on them? To make sure they're okay?"

He leaned against the wall again and crossed his arms. "Who looks after them?"

"They live in abhorrent conditions. When we took them home, their mother was passed out in the back yard. Isn't there something that can be done for them? Can you do something to protect them?"

With a slight eye roll and a quiet groan, "I'll inform Social Services that you've registered a complaint about the living conditions and let them take it from there. Maybe they'll be taken to a foster home somewhere. Happy now?"

"Maybe. As long as it's a really nice foster home. And the boys must stay together. That's most important."

The detective stood up again. "Your two minutes are up. Good day." He abruptly turned on his heel and walked quickly down the hall, disappearing into one of the doors.

Leona stood in the hallway, letting police personnel walk around her. The feeling was definite now. She didn't like him. She stomped her foot. He was arrogant and unhelpful and seemingly determined to throw roadblocks in the way of finding her necklace and ring. He didn't seem the least bit interested in protecting those boys. Wasn't that what police did? Protect the helpless? His methods and lack of caring seemed contrary to the way she thought police ought to do things.

As she walked to the minivan, she felt like she was being watched. She turned around to look, but saw nothing at first other than the usual scurry around the station. Moving mini blinds in a window caught her attention. Had someone been peering out of them, watching her? A shudder passed through her and she hurried along.

"How did it go?" Betty was cleaning the kitchen and getting ready to bake more cookies. "We've been worried."

Leona poured herself a cup of coffee and leaned against the countertop. "Not good."

Clarence was sitting at the dining table watching Betty work. He cleared his throat. "We've been talking and we think that maybe we're getting in too deep. This is starting to get dangerous."

Betty slid a baking sheet topped with cookie dough into the oven. She turned to face her sister. "I had a hard time getting out of bed this morning. I'm so sore from yesterday I can hardly move." She rubbed her backside and giggled lightly. "Your breakfast is in the refrigerator."

Leona laid her purse on the cabinet and got her plastic-wrapped eggs and strip of bacon out of the refrigerator. She knew what Betty meant. Her shoulder and hip hurt from yesterday too. Getting out of bed had been more painful than usual. If it hadn't been for two extra-strength pain reliever pills she took this morning, she doubted she would be functioning as well as she was.

As the leftovers from breakfast heated in the microwave, she told the two what had happened when she saw Detective Smythe and how she felt like someone was watching her when she left. "I don't like Smythe, but in spite of that, I didn't know who else to go to." The beep of the microwave signaled her to get her breakfast. "I couldn't sleep all night, thinking about those boys. They seemed so hungry and the place was so dirty. It's a wonder they aren't ill."

Betty nodded. "They seemed pretty healthy, but after seeing the way they dug into those cookies, I knew they were hungry. They grabbed those cookies like they hadn't eaten for days. That's why I'm making more. Maybe we can run them by later."

Clarence stood up, the first indication of energy from him today. "We should do better. Let's take them good healthy food. Let's call the church group and go help them out."

Leona held up her hand as she swallowed a bite. "Wait. We took them food yesterday. Their mother is in no shape to make sure they are fed. Today we should take food to Miz Molly and she could see that they ate properly. She's a much more caring person who is trying her best to raise her grandchildren. She's the one we should help and in turn she'll help the boys."

Betty let out a cry of glee. "Marvelous idea! Miz Molly came to our rescue. We need to return the good deed."

Leona finished the last of her lunch as Betty took the sheet of cookies out of the oven and slid another one in. At last, a sense of purpose had returned to her life. "Clarence, why don't you start the phone tree."

11

By the next morning, the church group members parked in front of Miz Molly's house with a boatload of cleaning supplies, food, and a few new household items. Miz Molly came outside and stood in front of her door. With her arms across her muumuu-covered chest and her bare feet spread across the width of the door, she made a formidable barrier.

"Why're y'all here?"

Betty led the negotiations. "Miz Molly, the day before yesterday you helped us out of a bad situation. Today we're here with our church group to return the favor and help you out with a few things." She held up a sack of groceries and a box of donuts. "We brought a few items we thought you might need, a few cleaning items—we'll help clean if you'd like—and screening fabric to repair your front door." She signaled for George to lift the materials up.

Miz Molly cocked her head and looked out the sides of her narrowed eyes. "I didn't ask for charity. I take care of my own."

Leona stepped forward. "It's not charity. It's repayment to you for your kindness. And…" she looked at the ground hoping the right words would come to her, "…to ask you to keep an eye on Doran, Jaden, and Tiger. They need a safe haven sometimes. And someone…" The words she longed to speak were caught before they could cause harm, "someone like you to guide them and teach them that they can have a better life. I believe you can do that."

Miz Molly's face softened a little and she spoke with less of a growl. "I don't run a foster home. I got my hands full with my own grandkids."

Leona's heart sank a little. This wasn't working out like she'd planned. "I know. Look, we didn't mean to impose. My thoughts were only for those boys. For some reason, I find myself attached to them." She tittered quietly. "I can't stand the thought of them not having a place to go when things at their house get out of hand."

Miz Molly uncrossed her arms and narrowed her stance. An uneasy quiet settled over the group as she eyed them. "You say you brought food?"

"Yes, we did!" Betty piped up as she started the procession up the front step. She introduced the church group to Miz Molly as they went through the door. Nods were given all around. The men stayed outside and began measuring the screen material for her screen door.

Inside, a small girl named Kendra and a toddler boy named Zilo sat on a stained ragged sofa in front of the TV, their hands frozen in mid-air above their cereal boxes. They watched wide-eyed as the army of strangers invaded their hovel.

The living room was so tiny that only Leona, Betty, Irene and Carly could fit in there. Betty carried the bag of groceries into the kitchen. She called to the children on the sofa to come in there. They obeyed and shortly returned to their places on the sofa with a donut in each hand.

Miz Molly directed the chaos and told Kendra to go get the boys. The other ladies put their cleaning supplies on the small table and the worn countertops. The floor under their feet sagged in places and creaked when they walked over it.

Carly tiptoed in. With a scrunched up face, she quickly

set her bag down and put a tissue over her mouth. "I've not been feeling well so I think I'll go out to the car so I don't make anyone else sick."

Even behind the tissue on her face, Leona could tell Carly's face was scrunched up in disgust. Carly backed out of the kitchen and quickly left the house.

The remaining faces were red, one with embarrassment and the others with anger. Leona had to bite her tongue to keep from saying things she didn't want Miz Molly to hear, but she'd release those words on Carly later. She stomped her foot hard and felt the floor give a little. *I better not do that again or I'll poke a hole in the floor*, she thought. Frustrated with herself and Carly, she twisted a package of sponges so hard that the package flew open and sponges went all over. She shut her eyes as she felt her face turn a deeper red. Even without looking, she could feel the eyes of the other women on her.

"I'd like to do that to her too."

Leona opened her eyes to see Betty with a smirk on her face, nodding.

"She deserves a good neck wringing." Betty laughed out loud as she bent down to pick up the sponges. The other joined in her laughter, even Miz Molly.

Irene put the sponges back into the grocery sack. "Please don't mind Carly, Miz Molly. She's a snob to everyone."

Miz Molly shrugged and held her head high. "I do my best to keep this place clean and fit for my grandkids. I make sure they go to school and we go to church on Sundays. They're good kids even though they ain't dressed in fancy clothes and we don't live in a fancy house." She crossed her arms, daring anyone to challenge her.

"And you do a great job!" Betty walked over to the lady and wrapped her arms around her large frame. "Those kids are lucky to have a caring grandmother to see after them."

Leona wiped a stray tear. "Let's get these things unpacked. We guessed about what to buy so if you don't want some of these things, we'll take them home. We're not trying to force anything on you." She pulled out cleaning wipes, toilet paper, paper towels, and cans of food. "This isn't charity. It's repayment of a kindness so please accept it with our thanks."

Miz Molly opened several kitchen cabinet doors that held a can of soup, three boxes of macaroni and cheese, a few plates and glasses, and one pan. "I thank you for that. I wish all my acts of kindness paid off this good." She let out a belly laugh and the others joined in.

Irene picked up the toilet paper and left to go find the bathroom. After a few moments, she returned. "I noticed you have a bucket under the bathroom sink. I told Nick to bring his plumber tools so he could fix it. He used to be a plumber so he knows how to do it. It'll be good as new."

Miz Molly's eyes grew damp. "We'd like that. If he fixes it, I don't have to get onto my grandkids when they forget to empty the bucket. I'll have to find another chore for them to do. Gotta keep them busy and outta trouble. Could he look at the leak under the sink in here too?" She opened the bottom cabinet door to reveal another pail with standing water in it.

Nick walked in carrying a large sack in one hand and a tool box in the other. "Here's the bread. Now where's that leak?"

Doran, Jaden, and Tiger came bouncing in the house behind Kendra, excited to see what was going on. Leona presented each one of them with a set of new pajamas which put big grins on their faces, along with some for Kendra and Zilo.

Kendra looked at them and went to her grandmother. "Grandma, T-bone and his gang are across the street. They hollered at us when we came back."

Leona heard Miz Molly suck in a breath. "Y'all need to go now. T-bone looks for trouble wherever he can find it

and he won't like ya'll being here. Run home now. Scat!"
She waved her large arms like she was shooing flies.

Betty stood fixed to the floor. "But we ordered pizza to
be delivered later."

When the word 'pizza' was spoken, all of the kids
started shouting the word and dancing with glee. Miz Molly
tried to calm them down, but the surprise had been
revealed. She would be hosting a pizza party.

Nick brought his tool box into the kitchen. "Got the
bathroom leak fixed. Just needed sealing up. You shouldn't
have any trouble now. Let's look at this one." He set his
tool box on the floor and opened the cabinet. "I need room
to work so you women should go supervise the screen door
repairs."

Miz Molly fidgeted nervously. "How long's it gonna
take?"

"Depends on what's wrong." Nick got on the floor and
opened the door.

Miz Molly paced a little, then said, "All right. Go ahead
and fix it. I want it done."

The women moved to the living room where the kids
were watching TV. Miz Molly rubbed her forehead. "T-
bone won't like this. He could cause trouble for me. And
you." She looked at Leona with narrowed, knowing eyes.
"He came to see me after ya'll left yesterday. He don't like
you, so you need to watch out. Stay on your side of town."

Leona's heart fluttered with fearful butterflies. The
warning was not given lightly and it wasn't taken lightly
either. The last thing she wanted to do was put this woman
and the kids in harm's way. The advice was the same as
everyone else had given her: let it go.

"We'll leave as soon as the pizza arrives and we pay for
it."

Miz Molly nodded and went outside with Irene and
Betty to watch George cutting the screen mesh to size for
the door. Leona was glad they would be out there for a

while. She wanted to talk to Doran while she had the chance.

Leona took the oldest boy aside and asked him for more information about T-bone. The boy was reluctant at first to say anything, but once he said a little, the floodgates opened. T-bone was the head of a gang that lived in that house where they'd first seen him. His friend that had been with him was his brother. He was the head of a gang that was pushing people around in the neighborhood. He, Miz Molly, and Miz Han, Miz Molly's neighbor, had a truce. He stayed on his side of the street and they stayed on theirs. Leona asked him where T-bone got his money. The boy didn't know, but lately there'd been more activity there than usual. A strange man was seen going in and out, but he didn't know who it was.

Nick declared he was done in the kitchen and went outside with the others. Leaving the kids with the TV, Leona followed him out just in time to see a strange woman staggering down the street, followed by a confused looking man. Both had blood-shot eyes. She looked around and screamed out, "Who 'er you and what the…"

Unseen, Doran stood behind Leona and screamed out at the same time she was yelling, "Mom, watch your language!" He stepped around Leona and ran over to his raving mother. He tried to calm her, but she looked at him with unfocused eyes. She wavered on her feet, then let out a barrage of profanities that shook the trees.

The church members covered their ears and said prayers out loud. George told Clarence to take Betty and Irene to the cars as he picked up his tools. Nick stood by Leona, with his hand on her elbow, ready to guide her safely away. The other kids came out of the house to see the commotion, but stood near the door.

Doran came running back to Leona and looked up at her with sad eyes. "Miz Leona, you go home now. We'll stay here until Momma's doing yard work." He turned and yelled, "Come on, Tiger and Jaden. Momma's calling."

Leona had trouble catching her breath and tears stung her eyes. These poor boys! Her heart ached for them. "Why don't you come to my house until your mother calms down?"

"No, Miz Leona," Jaden said. "You're the reason she's mad. It's better not to make her madder than she is." He turned to go, pulling his brother and cousin behind him.

Seeing the quiet conversation, Miz Molly walked up to join in. "Doran is right. You need to go now. The boys can stay here for a while. She'll listen to me. You like pizza, don't you, Doran?" A beaming smile and wide grin gave his answer. She turned to Leona, "Ya'll go now before you attract any more trouble or attention."

Leona's heart sunk, but she knew it was the right thing to do. She nodded. "We never meant to cause problems."

Miz Molly nodded. "I know, but you don't belong here. Go back to your side of town."

Tears stung Leona's eyes and she nodded. She called out to the group, "Time to go! George, leave money for the pizza."

George approached Miz Molly with his wallet out. He handed her a $10 bill. "It's already paid for, but this is a tip for the delivery boy." Miz Molly took it, staring at it like a hungry dog looks at a bone.

Leona touched her arm to draw her out of the spell. "We'll go now, but you call me if you need anything. Or if the boys need anything." She gave Miz Molly a card with her phone number written on it. The church group got in their cars and left Miz Milly and the kids standing in the yard while the boys' mother raged in the street and T-bone watched them and gestured while they drove away.

Leona wiped away a tear as she drove. Her jaw muscles started to ache a little from being worked so hard. *I'm won't forget those boys. I'll come back later to make sure they're okay.*

12

At breakfast the next morning, Clarence sat in his usual spot eating breakfast with the sisters. He cleared his throat after a sip of coffee. "I've been thinking, things aren't going the way we thought they would. We're going to places where we've never been before and we've been pushed around..."

Betty cleared her throat... "I don't remember picking you up off the ground. And since when have you become a Korean vet? You were in high school when it ended."

Clarence gave her a don't-interrupt-me glare. "We've been in parts of town that we normally avoid. We had to listen to the ravings of a foul woman. And we've made no progress toward finding your things, Leona. I think it's an indication that we should back off and let the police handle it."

Betty put down her tea cup. "I agree with you, Clarence. I think we've bitten off more than we can chew. How do you feel about it, Leona?"

Leona pushed her plate of fruit and toast away from her. "I've had the same thoughts. I think it's time to bring in backup. I'm going to see Tristan today."

"Tristan?" Betty asked. "How is a lawyer going to help out?"

Leona shuffled a few toast crumbs with her thumb. "Now that we know about T-bone, I'll call Tristan later this morning and see if there's anything we can do to move this investigation along. You want to go too?"

Clarence nodded as he grabbed his walker and headed toward the door. "I shouldn't even be involved with this. My house wasn't robbed. Right now, I'm tired! I'm going to take a nap." The door shut behind him.

Leona looked at Betty. Her confused face mirrored her own. "A nap? We haven't been up that long."

Betty got up and took her dishes to the sink. "Leona, maybe we should stay out of it. Clarence is right. Things are getting worse and we're too old for this. After getting pushed down and yesterday's episode with the boys' mother, I think we all need a day of rest, don't you?"

Leona stirred the last few bites of breakfast around on her plate, then got up and took her dishes to the sink too. "Maybe. But now I'm thinking about those boys. Maybe I should file a report about their mother and the living conditions. I mainly want to ask Tristan about that. What kind of guarantee do we have that they'd stay together and go into a good foster home. I hear terrible things about them, but there's got to be some good ones out there somewhere. I mean, if I do file an official complaint and they get stuck in a lousy foster home or get separated, I haven't done them any favors. At least where they are, they have Miz Molly and they're together."

Betty rinsed the dishes and put them in the dishwasher. "Those boys have really stolen your heart." She smiled at Leona who smiled back at her. She took off her apron that covered her lilac sweat suit.

"I guess they have. It's the teacher in me. I love children, and it breaks my heart to see them in that bad home situations. In spite of that, they seem to be nice boys. If we could save them from all the bad influences around them, maybe they'd grow up to be fine citizens." Leona put her dishes in the dishwasher and shut the door. "But first, I'll work my crossword puzzle and nap in my chair."

Later that day, the trio sat in Tristan's office, hoping for good news. Leona detailed their visits with T-bone and Miz Molly. His raised eyebrows and gaping mouth through the whole explanation made Leona wonder if he even believed her. After she finished, he sat motionless for a full minute before sitting back in his chair to rock slightly and tap his fingertips together. Leona watched him closely. He seemed unable to sit still for more than a second. Something on him was always moving. His legs, his chair, his hands. He was like a perpetual motion toy. Leona resisted the urge to frown. She looked down at her hands so she wouldn't have to watch the jittering.

"I'm going to be brutally frank with you," he began. "I think you need to butt out."

Leona's mouth fell open. Her jaw moved up and down while her brain struggled to find words to send out that expressed her disbelief.

Tristan didn't wait for her brain to sort the matter out. "Let's put this in perspective. Your house was robbed and that in and of itself is a traumatic event. Your space was violated and you lost items that you value. You've replaced many of the things you lost, but there are two particular items you want returned. Right so far?" The trio nodded without saying a word.

Tristan continued. "In your search for these two items, you've been places you've never been before and probably have no business being. Right?" The trio nodded. "You've been threatened, you've been accosted, you've been royally cursed at. Right?"

The trio nodded without saying a word.

Tristan continued. "You've possibly put a nice grandmother into harm's way because her neighbors know she's working with you, and you are working with the police. Her safety and the safety of her grandchildren could be in jeopardy because you want to find two small items that mean a lot to you. Do I have that down right?" Leona gulped and nodded her head.

Clarence pointed to Leona. "She's the leader of our gang. Betty and I just go along to make sure she's okay. So don't blame us."

Tristan frowned as he rocked in his chair. "I'm not blaming anyone. T-bone's gang won't differentiate between Leona and you two. In their eyes, you're all alike." He tapped his fingers together as he studied their faces. "You asked for my advice, and I'm giving it. Let the police handle it."

Leona rolled her eyes. "You don't understand how much Joe's ring and Mother's necklace mean to me."

"Enough to endanger other people?" Tristan stared at Leona long and hard. For once, he sat still, waiting for her response.

Leona hung her head and said softly, "I didn't intend for that to happen."

"But it did. And are you prepared to further endanger those folks? From what you've said, if T-bone gets mad at any of his neighbors, he could make their lives miserable. Is that worth it? Will you trade the ring for the wellbeing of others?"

Leona felt as low as a gnat's knees. As much as she hated to admit it, this young whippersnapper was right. Her attempt to be her own investigator was a miserable failure. If anyone ever got hurt due to her bumbling efforts, she'd never forgive herself.

Tristan started rocking in his chair again. "I think you need to give it up. The ring is gone. The necklace is gone. But you have your health, your memories, and your friends so you're still a lucky woman."

Leona opened her purse and found a tissue. She held it between both hands, tearing it into tiny strips and letting them fall back into her open purse. "Are the police stopping their work on the case?"

"The investigation is ongoing," he said. He was slightly twirling his chair with his elbows on the armrests and his fingertips tapping together.

"If I'd wanted to hear that, I'd have gone back to the police station." Leona looked up at her fidgety lawyer. *Maybe I can intimidate him. He's so young and I'm so— never mind.* "Have you done anything to move the case forward?"

"Like what?"

Betty moved in her seat. "Like Perry Mason does. He has an investigator, Paul Walters, to move things along. Don't you have someone like that who can go look around for clues?"

Tristan leaned forward against his desk. "Like who?"

Betty slapped her chest and gasped, "What do they teach you in those fancy lawyer schools? Don't you know who Perry Mason is?"

Clarence patted Betty on the arm to calm her. "Now, Betty, Perry Mason is a TV show, not a real person."

"But I'd think all lawyers would want to be like him! He won all his cases."

"Only on TV." Clarence patted her arm more. "Don't lose touch with reality. This is real. Perry Mason is not."

Betty gave Clarence a don't-patronize-me look, then turned back to Tristan. "I'm sorry, dear boy, but at least Perry Mason tried to help his clients. You haven't done anything."

Tristan sat back in his chair and continued his slight rocking. "I've made inquiries into the status of the case. That's about all I can do. Everything is in the hands of the police."

Leona's shoulders slumped. Those weren't the words she wanted to hear.

Betty reached over and patted her shoulder. "You've done all you can do. The ring is gone, sister. Give up the chase."

Leona and her gang left the lawyer's office more discouraged than ever. "Go home," he'd said. "Go home and be patient. Let justice take its course." He promised to keep them informed on the investigation's progress. Betty and Clarence didn't seem to mind going home. They chatted cheerfully on the way, driving Leona to the edge of screaming.

Leona knew that she couldn't sit around and wait for something to happen. Not quite a week had passed since the crime, and every passing moment pushed her farther away from finding her mother's necklace and Joe's ring. Joe's ring. It made her heart hurt to think his ring might be melted down for its gold. No, she would cling to hope. She didn't care about justice. Justice was only interesting in finding who did this and not in recovering the ring. It was up to her to do that.

Let justice take its course, but don't expect me to sit at home and do nothing to find Joe's ring. I'm going back to work.

The week was busy with moving back into the house and getting everything back to normal. Betty stayed in the kitchen for hours, baking and cooking. Clarence sat at the table and watched her work. Leona had called Miz Molly a couple of times to check on the boys.

Leona was restless. She'd made a plan and come Friday, when the flea market was open again, she'd go back. Answers to her questions may be there if she could pry them out of Tattoo Man. He could tell her which gold dealer had Joe's ring. Once she found that out, she'd go there and hope that it was still a ring and not a glob of metal.

Friday morning dawned bright and warm. Leona offered to take her companions out for lunch. Never suspecting a thing, they accepted and came along for the ride. Once lunch was over, they quickly discovered her underlying purpose.

"Where are you taking us?" Clarence asked as Leona turned the minivan toward the flea market.

"I'm going back to talk to Tattoo Man. I think he knew more than he was saying and I'm going to ask."

Clarence didn't wait to clear his throat. "Have you lost your mind?" Clarence bellowed from the backseat. "I want to go home!"

Betty patted her arm softly. "Now, Leona, you heard what Tristan said. Let's go home and you'll feel better. Be patient."

"I've been patient! No more. I want Joe's ring back before it gets melted down and time's awasting!"

The whole way to the flea market, Clarence continued to voice his disapproval of her mission and his desire to go home. Betty offered Leona a cookie, but when she refused, she stayed quiet, looking out the window without saying anything.

After Leona parked, she gathered her purse and turned to the others. "Who's going with me?"

Betty took a bag of cookies out of her tote and opened her door to get out. Both ladies looked back at Clarence, who was frowning.

He crossed his arms. "I don't think you should go. It's a bad idea to go back to where you obviously weren't wanted the first time."

"Fine. Stay here." She turned the key enough to crack the windows so the air could circulate. She took the keys out and put them on the center console in case Clarence needed them to roll the windows down or needed to lock the van if he left to find a restroom.

"You'll be sorry. You'll wish I'd come when he yells at you again. I won't be there to protect you."

"I'll be the one doing the yelling today. I'm fed up with the whole situation. So you're staying then?"

Clarence made no move, but eyed the keys. "Maybe I'll just drive myself home."

Leona picked the keys up and put them in her purse. "Be back in a bit." Leona got out with Betty close behind.

The two ladies made their way through the maze of booths and customers. Leona saw Tattoo Man talking with a customer as she walked up to the jewelry case. He looked her way and made a face. He took a step backward and Leona was afraid he was going to run. He picked up an item and showed it to his customers. Leona breathed a sigh of relief. She looked through his jewelry display and out of the corner of her eye, saw him frown. Nothing in the case looked familiar. Joe's ring wasn't there and neither was her mother's necklace.

He came over and whispered out of the corner of his mouth, "Why are you here? I told you not to come back."

"I know. I'm just checking back. Has anyone offered to sell you a gold band?" She took her mother's photo from her purse. "Or tried to sell you this necklace?"

Tattoo Man didn't even look at the photo. "No. Happy? Now go away."

"It's not good business to run customers off like that. Plus it's rude." Tattoo Man, Betty, and Leona spun around to see Smythe standing there with a smug look on his face. He leaned against the glass cabinet. "Why don't you tell her the truth? That you saw her things and already sold them."

Tattoo Man's face paled and his mouth fell open. He stuttered, looking for an excuse. Smythe held up his hand to silence him.

"I talked to the gold buyer downtown and found out that you sold him several gold wedding bands last week. It's likely her missing ring was one of them."

Leona felt like the room was about to start spinning out of control. She grabbed the case to keep her balance. Betty reached out to steady her.

Detective Smythe put his hands on his hips, pushing his suit jacket behind his hands. His shoulder holster and pistol were visible with his stance. "I'm sorry to tell you this way, but your ring's been destroyed."

"I didn't know any of them was stolen," Tattoo Man blurted out. "People bring me their stuff and tell me it's theirs. How can I know if it was stolen? You can't arrest me for that!" He started to back away and Smythe grabbed his arm to prevent him from leaving.

"You hear that, Leona?" Detective Smythe asked her. "The ring is gone so you can stop looking for it. Understand? Go home. Grieve. Learn to live with it."

Leona felt the words stab at her heart. Her brain wouldn't work right and she didn't know how to respond. Things swirled in her head. Anger. Confusion. Grief. Fear. Loathing. She gripped the case so tightly that it hurt her hand and the pain brought her out of her trance.

"Thank you for your time, Smythe," Betty said softly. Leona steadied herself before letting go of the jewelry case. "I'll take my sister home now."

Just then, a young woman walked in from the back. She went up to Tattoo Man and told him she'd finished unpacking the boxes. Leona stared at the woman's neck. Her mother's necklace hung down. The patina of the elaborate chain gave it away, along with the ruby twinkling under the florescent lights.

"That's my mother's necklace!" Leona yelled, pointing at the girl. She dashed around the jewelry case as quickly as her legs would carry her. With outstretched hands, she lunged at the girl who shrunk back. Leona got her mother's photo out of her purse again and waved it around. "Smythe, that's my necklace!"

The girl's eyes widened and she looked to Tattoo Man to see what she should do. She stepped behind him and turned slightly, getting ready to run.

Detective Smythe stepped between Leona and the girl. "We have to be sure," he said as he pushed his way by Leona. "Young lady, where did you get that necklace?"

The young woman's demeanor changed in an instant. She put one hand on her hip and flipped her head back. "Who's this old lady? And what's she talking about? I got this necklace from my boyfriend. It's mine!"

"Your boyfriend's a thief! Arrest her, Detective!" Leona reached around Smythe for the necklace, but the girl agilely jumped away from her reach. She held her hand on the necklace, blocking it from Leona's view. She spun on her heels and ran out the back. Leona tried to follow her, but Betty and Smythe held her back.

"She has my necklace!" Leona was writhing, trying to free herself from their grips. "Why aren't you chasing her? She's got my mother's necklace! Go get her!"

"Stop it!" Smythe yelled at her as he struggled with her, "Or I'll run you in for disturbing the peace!"

Leona stopped fighting him and looked around. Every eye in the building was on her, staring and wondering. Even Tattoo Man and Betty looked at her like she'd lost her mind. She felt her face redden. She tried to pull away and Smythe loosened his grip. "I'm sorry," she said quietly. "Why are you still standing here? She's a suspect in the robbery of our home! Do your job!" Her voice was getting louder and more desperate.

Detective Smythe released her arm and got in her face. "You're a piece of work, you know it? I told you to leave this to me, but noooo. You keep getting in my way. What do I have to do to keep you out of my business?" He pulled back, looking thoroughly exasperated.

"You could have found my Joe's ring before it was destroyed," she said defiantly. She pointed toward the back where the girl had disappeared. "That girl has my mother's necklace and you know it. It matches this photo that I showed you days ago. Yet here you stand holding on to an old woman. I'm the victim here! She's the criminal. Why don't you do your duty and catch her? Get my necklace and ring back and then I'll leave you alone."

Smythe jabbed his finger at her face. "You don't know what you're dealing with! Back off before you get someone hurt!"

Leona grabbed his finger and pushed it away. The two squared off against each other, not blinking or giving ground. The tension around them was so thick that it pushed Tattoo Man and Betty a step back. Betty quickly opened her purse and pulled out a cookie-filled bag.

"Cookies anyone?" she squeaked. "Things always look better over cookies."

Symthe blinked and snatched the bag from Betty's hand. He stuffed a cookie in his mouth and grabbed three more before handing the bag back to Betty. He walked through Tattoo Man's booth and went out the back entrance after the girl, leaving Leona glaring after him.

"Come on, Leona," Betty said, returning the cookie bag to her purse. "There's nothing else here to look for."

"Yes, there is!" Leona ran out the back, following behind Smythe and the girl.

13

An hour later, Leona made her way back to her minivan. Smythe and the girl had disappeared. Her feet hurt from walking around for a solid hour and she limped slightly as she approached the minivan. The glares sent her way from the minivan caused her to stop in her tracks for an instant. It was her punishment for dragging them along and there was no escaping it. She got into the hostility-filled vehicle.

On the drive home, little was said. Clarence fell asleep in the backseat. Betty looked out the side window. Leona fumed. Her mother's necklace had been so close, she could have grabbed it off that girl's neck. If only she'd been quicker. If only she would have chased that girl as soon as she left. If only Joe hadn't died.

The worst part was that the girl looked familiar, but she couldn't remember where she'd seen her. Somewhere unexpected and not too long ago. But where? She racked her brain, but nothing useful came. She let out a soft growl, frustrated by her not-what-it-used-to-be memory.

When she turned into her driveway, Doran, Jaden, and Tiger were playing in the yard. Doran seemed enthralled with her rose bushes under the bedroom window, but ran back to the porch steps when he saw the minivan. Jaden and Tiger were rolling around in the lush grass, oblivious to their arrival. When they heard the minivan turn into the driveway, they jumped up and ran to Doran. She stopped short of the garage and turned the motor off. The boys stood up, smiling and waving.

"What on earth?" Betty said as she opened her door. "They're a long ways from home." She called out to Clarence who roused from his nap.

He stirred, cleared his throat, and took off his seatbelt. "About time we got home. I need to find a new taxi driver." He got out and hung on to the minivan until Leona brought his walker. As she gave him his walker, Leona pointed out that they had company. He squeaked his way to the front porch where the boys were sitting. He called out to them as he started up the ramp. "You boys are a long ways from home. How'd you get here?"

"We ran," Tiger said. "We're good runners."

"You got a squeaky wheel," Jaden said as he pointed at the offending part.

"Oh, so now you're an expert in fixing things?" Clarence raised his eyebrows. "I don't hear any squeak." He pushed his walker forward and backwards a bit. "This works just fine."

Tiger ran over to Leona and gave her a hug around her middle, followed by the other boys who expected hugs too. Leona was more than happy to give them before they went to Betty expecting the same. They had their new clothes on. Tiger's pants were a little too big, but someone had fashioned a belt out of rope which held them up. On their feet were shoes that should have been discarded long ago. Leona tsked. She'd have to take them to the store to get new ones.

Leona sat in her wicker chair. The boys piled on the porch swing. "What are you doing here? How did you find out where I lived?"

Tiger shouted out as he danced around, "We went to the

liberry! Doran knows how to use the computer!"

"I know how to Google." Doran beamed with pride of his accomplishment. "You can get maps from it."

The elderly trio looked at each other in amazement. "Wow!" said Betty for all of them. "That's impressive! You're a very smart boy, Doran."

The look on the boy's face after being paid a compliment caused Leona to almost tear up. Obviously, the boy didn't hear kind words often and he absorbed them like a sponge. Leona hoped he'd cling to those words when his life was less calm.

Leona shook her head slightly to focus. "That answers the how. Why are you here?"

"Our mother told us to come tell you that she's sorry for the way she acted when you were there last time," Doran said. "She liked that you bought clothes for us. Miz Molly sent some of the food you give her to our house. She says that's real Christian of you."

"She wanted to call you, but we wanted to come see you," said Tiger.

"Does she know you're here?" Leona gave them a hard look.

Doran shrugged. "I dunno. We didn't tell her. She was busy."

Leona dug through her purse to find her cell phone. "How about we call her and tell her we'll bring you home." She gave her phone to Doran. If he could work a computer, he would no trouble calling his mom on her phone.

"Miz Betty," Tiger said shyly. "You got cookies?"

Betty laughed. "Do I have cookies? Of course I do! I'm the cookie lady! I'll get them and we'll have a picnic on the porch."

Leona watched the boys play on the porch swing. The boys had triggered the right memory. She'd seen that girl on the front step of T-bone's house. She was the one hanging around him and Baggy Pants. She smiled. She'd offer to take the boys home and after dropping them off, she'd go by T-bone's house to check on the girl. She would offer to buy the necklace back. She'd lost Joe's ring, but she wouldn't lose that necklace.

The boys marched into their kitchen with three bags of groceries, smiling like they were carrying precious gifts of gold. From the look of the garbage can in the kitchen, the trash around the house had been quickly picked up. The carpet looked a century old, worn and holey. The drabness and deteriorated interior were depressing to Leona. Her heart gave her a twinge of guilt for living so well while they lived in such dire conditions.

The boys' mother, Lila, seemed mostly sober as the boys showed her what they brought home. The slight trembling in her hands and her bloodshot eyes exposed her tenuous condition. She thanked them for the clothes and the extra food.

Jaden's smile lit up the room. "Mom! They gave us $10 each and we got to buy whatever we wanted! Look what I bought!" He pulled two boxes of cereal, two big cans of spaghetti and three cans of chili.

"We planned it out," Doran said as he unloaded his hot dog buns, frankfurters, and lunch meat. He helped Tiger put both of his sacks on the table. Tiger climbed into a chair and pulled out bread and three bags of potato chips.

"Not enough veggies in the mix," Betty said as she added a large bag of cookies to the pile. "They didn't seem too interested in those."

"And look at our new shoes!" Tiger held up his foot, showing his brightly colored shoes that flashed each time he took a step. "Now I can run like the wind!" He ran around the small living room making wind sounds with his mouth.

Their mother gave a weak smile. She swayed slightly and her red eyes seemed to redden more. Jaden went and hugged her around her legs as she stroked his hair. "Thanks for what you've done. I like seeing my boys happy. We have a hard life here, but my boys are good kids."

Leona held out her arms and they ran to her. "Yes, they are." She gathered them in a big hug and said, "We should go now. Boys, eat well and be good!"

As the trio drove away, Leona turned the corner and stopped in front of T-bone's house. "I finally remembered where I had seen that girl with Mother's necklace. She was hanging around with T-bone. I'm going to see if she's here and maybe I can persuade her to give me the necklace. Or maybe I'll let President Grant do the talking for me." She waved the $50 bill around before stuffing it in her pants pocket.

"Are you nuts, Leona?" Clarence said from the backseat. "This is not a good part of town. He pointed to the house. "That dump of a house is not a place an old woman should go alone, especially at dusk."

Betty joined in with Clarence, "He's right, dear. Maybe we should call Smythe."

"He wouldn't do a thing. He didn't even chase that girl after we saw her. No, I'm not calling him." Leona opened her door. "I'm going in. You can stay or go with me, I don't care." She got out and walked around the minivan. She heard the minivan doors open and Betty clanging Clarence's walker around while trying to get it out. She paused to let them catch up before she started up the crumbling sidewalk.

Clarence's squeaky wheel was like a car alarm, announcing their presence to the neighborhood. A dog barked nearby and booming music beat its way down the street. They didn't see or hear anyone as they crept toward the door.

"I wonder if anyone is home?" Betty whispered.

"What ch'all doing over yonder?" a voice boomed out across the quiet neighborhood.

The sound sent bolts of fear through the elderly trio. They jerked around to look behind them. There, silhouetted in the doorway of her home, Miz Molly stood.

Leona grabbed her chest to stop her heart from racing. She waved her arm, hoping Miz Molly could see it in the dim lights of evening. Miz Molly waved back and came toward them. She stopped on her side of the street.

"What ch'all up to?" She stood with her hands on her hips.

"Wait here," Leona told Betty and Clarence as she took off toward Miz Molly. After briefly explaining her intentions, she persuaded Miz Molly to come along with her.

As Leona and Miz Molly went past Clarence, he muttered, "So now she's roped you into trouble too."

"Hush, Clarence." Leona and Miz Molly climbed the steps and knocked at the door. It swung open by itself at the first knock to reveal a mostly empty room. The faded paint on the walls and the washed-out color of the threadbare carpet emphasized the neglected state of the structure.

"Yoo hoo," Leona called out, "Anyone home?" She waited, but heard nothing in response. She took a step inside.

"Leona, get out of there!" Clarence whispered loudly. "You're breaking and entering."

"No, I'm not! The door swung open on its own."

Miz Molly took Leona's elbow. "I think we should listen to Clarence."

"No!" Leona said gruffly. "We won't go in very far. Just enough to see if anyone's home."

Leona stepped just inside the door and looked around the small living room that opened into a hallway. "Yoo hoo!" She waited for an answer, but heard nothing. She took another step inside. "I'm Leona Templeton, here with Miz Molly. I'm looking for the young lady that lives here. I want to buy that necklace she was wearing today." No response. "I don't mean to intrude. I just want to talk." No response. "Is anyone here?"

"No one's home," Miz Molly said from the doorway. "Come on out of there and let's go to my house."

Leona waved her off. The streetlights dimly lit the small room as she tiptoed across the living room and looked into the kitchen. Seeing nothing, she turned around and crept back into the living room. In the dim lights, something in the hallway caught her eye. On the floor, a pair of legs stuck out of another room. Thinking about the boys' mother doing yard work, she went to see if the person needed help. As she got to the doorway, she could see inside. The girl she was looking for was lying there, with a pool of blood around her head like a halo. Lifeless eyes stared at the ceiling. Her mother's necklace was still around her neck.

14

Blue and red emergency lights lit up the crowd gathered along the yellow crime-scene tape that encircled T-bone's house. Police buzzed in and out of the house like bees around a hive. More yellow tape circled Leona's minivan, its occupants nowhere to be seen. Doran, Jaden, and Tiger stood behind the yellow tape, kept there by the vigilant eye of a policewoman after their many attempts to run into the house.

Inside the dirty house, Leona sat on the edge of a chair gathered from the other room. Betty had wiped it with tissues from her purse, but to no avail. Clarence had protested when ordered to sit in another chair, claiming the dirt would never come off his pants. Betty and Miz Molly sat on the dirty sofa against one wall.

Smythe came up to the Leona and stood with his arms crossed, shaking his head and tsking at her. "Seems strange to me that you're here with a dead body. A body that has your mother's necklace on it." He leaned down to get in Leona's face. "Just how bad did you want your mother's necklace back?"

Leona's mouth fell open, then her eyes narrowed in anger. She leaned forward to narrow the space between their faces so he would not mistake her answer. "Not bad enough to kill someone. I would never do that. And you know it!"

He straightened up. "Last time I saw you, you were trying to get at her. Did you follow her here and kill her because she wouldn't give the necklace back?"

Leona let out a hurrumph. "Now you're being ridiculous! Of course not! Quit trying to make me look like a murderer because I'm not." She crossed her arms and looked the other way. "I spent the afternoon shopping. And Miz Molly can testify that the girl was dead when I got here."

Clarence cried out, "She didn't follow her here. We went home first. We're only here because we took some boys home who live in this area. Leona stopped here to see that girl and offer to buy her necklace. This girl was already dead when we got here. We. Didn't. Do. It!" He banged his walker on the floor for emphasis.

"What're the name of the boys?"

Leona hesitated. She and Miz Molly exchanged glances that confirmed they were reading each other's minds. Leona didn't want to involve them in this, and from the look on Miz Molly's face, she agreed with Leona. Nothing good could come of it. She'd take a lot of blame before she'd hand them over to Smythe. "I'd rather not say. They're innocent kids that had nothing to do with any of this."

The veins on Smythe's neck started to bulge as he worked his jaw. He flexed his fists. He got so close to Leona's face that his breath ruffled her hair. "What were you really doing here? I want to know!" His voice echoed through the house.

Another man walked up next to Smythe and put his hand on his shoulder. Smythe stood up and walked away. The man pulled a badge from his coat pocket. "I'm Charlie Walters. Homicide and Major Crimes Division." He never took his eyes off of Leona when he said, "Miz Molly, you're free to go home. Thanks for your help."

Miz Molly got up and left without saying a word or giving a look at anyone. Leona closed her eyes and said a prayer. *Lord, bless Miz Molly and don't let me be fool enough to lose her as a friend.*

Charlie turned back to Leona. "You said you were in the neighborhood. Where did you go?"

Leona gave him the address.

"Why did you go there?"

"To take three little boys home. They'd come to see us and we brought them back."

"How did you end up here?"

Leona took a deep breath of exasperation. "I saw this lady earlier today at the flea market. She had my mother's necklace on. Detective Smythe was there so he can verify that. I couldn't remember where I'd seen this girl before, but I finally remembered. I'd seen her here. So, after I took the boys home, I stopped by to see if she'd sell the necklace to me. Miz Molly joined me to keep me safe. She did nothing. Betty and Clarence are here because I drug them along. That's the whole story and that's the honest truth."

Smythe rushed over and leaned over to get in Leona's face again. He yelled at the top of his lungs. "I think you're lying! You came here looking for T-bone. You think he robbed your house and sold that gold ring you've been looking for. You found out it had been melted down and you were angry. Very angry. Angry enough to kill!"

The other cops and investigators stopped to see what was going on. Smythe remained inches from Leona's face as she returned his glare. The battle of wills was intense.

"Here kitty kitty."

Leona was startled, but didn't break her eye contact with the detective. The intensity between them eased infinitesimally while both tried to figure out what was going on.

"Here kitty kitty."

Leona was the first to turn and look at Betty. Betty was bent forward on the sofa, holding her hand out. "Here kitty kitty."

The room fell silent. Everyone stared at her. She smiled sweetly and said, "You boys want some cookies? If you help me find my kitty, I'll let you have some."

Smythe looked at Leona with a question in his eyes. Leona shrugged.

The tension in the room lowered as the investigators chuckled before going about their business. Smythe stood back. Charlie stepped in front of him to talk to Leona. "We should talk to the boys you brought home. They might know what's been going on around here."

"They had nothing to do with this. I'd rather you left them alone."

Charlie shook his head. "They might have more information. We'll take good care of them."

Clarence glanced at Leona in a way that let her know that he was tired and wanted it all to end. "They live up the street a little ways. There's three of them. Doran, Jaden, and Tiger. They walked to our house so we drove them home."

Charlie stared at Clarence. "From here? That's a long walk." Clarence and Leona both shrugged when he looked at them for answers. "Why did they show up at your house?"

Clarence continued to lead. "We met them when we did some church work for Miz Molly. They showed up and we made friends with them. They walked over to Leona's house to thank us for the clothes we'd bought for them. If you ask me, I think the reason they came was for more of Betty's chocolate chip cookies. They're nice boys, especially considering the place they come from."

Charlie called Smythe over. "Take the cat lady here outside to find the boys. Ask them where they were tonight.

See if they can shed any more light on this."

As Smythe helped Betty up, she asked him, "Have you seen my kitty? He loves my cookies." In a short time, they returned and the word was given that the boys confirmed Clarence's story.

Charlie wrote a few notes in his notebook. "Okay, you can go, Leona, but don't leave town. You're still a person of interest in this."

Smythe heaved a sigh and ran his hand through his hair. His hands shook, but Leona could tell he was trying to hide it. His pacing and nervousness indicated he was a man under stress from something more than just solving a crime.

Leona rose from her seat and Betty helped Clarence get up. They shuffled through the living room and out into the night. A crowd was still gathered behind the yellow tape. The flashing lights made it hard to see the ground clearly and Clarence nearly fell after tripping on the uneven sidewalk. The boys ran up and grabbed him around the waist, trying to help him along. Once they got Clarence into the minivan, the ladies hugged the boys and told them to go home immediately.

Miz Molly stood at the curb in front of her house. She called the boys over to her. She told them loudly enough for Leona to hear that they would be staying with her for the night.

Leona tore the crime tape away from her minivan. She looked cross the street where Miz Molly was standing, hands on her hips, and shaking her head. Five little heads peered around her and she waved them back into the small house before she followed them in.

Leona's heart sank. The one person on this side of town whose respect she most desired was Miz Molly. From the looks of her reaction, she'd lost what little credibility she had with Miz Molly. She turned the ignition and pulled away from the curb. One day, she decided, she'd come back and make amends with the kind woman.

15

A slit of bright sunlight made its way across Leona's bed. It woke her when it reached her face, waking her faster than any alarm clock. The room seemed brighter than normal so she glanced at the clock to discover she'd overslept by an hour. She didn't care. She didn't want to get out of bed. She heard Betty stirring in the kitchen, but heard nothing from Clarence. *Oh yes*, she thought, *it's Sunday morning. The only morning he doesn't come over for breakfast.*

Sunday mornings used to be a joyful occasion. She and Joe would lie in bed and talk about the week ahead. Then they would go to church. There they would hear a wonderful sermon. After services, they'd join their church group friends to eat lunch at the best buffet in town.

Leona smiled as the memories tickled her heart. She looked over at the empty pillow next to her. No ring. And it would never be there again. It was now a lump of gold. Just like that lump that was forming in her throat. A tear ran down her cheek and into her ear. It tickled. When another tear followed, she used the edge of the sheet to wipe it away.

The grief over the loss of Joe and now his ring made her

heart hurt. Seeing her mother's favorite necklace around the neck of that poor girl in the pool of blood was more than she could bear. She'd been wrong to pursue it so relentlessly. Maybe it was her fault the girl was dead. All over a necklace and a ring. More tears followed and soon the sheet edge was wet.

The sound of a platter shattering shook her out of her pity party. Betty let out a cry of alarm and Leona jumped out of bed, stopping long enough to put on her slippers. Running into the kitchen in her nightgown, she saw Betty in her robe crying at the table. Relieved that she didn't find her on the floor with a heart attack, Leona sat beside her and hugged her shoulders.

"It's been a hard week, hasn't it," Leona said. She looked at the scattered pieces of a china plate Betty liked to put cookies on when serving to friends.

Betty nodded. "Let's rest today after church. There's nothing pressing to be done."

"No, there's not. Let's have a 'normal' day. After lunch, we'll read the paper, maybe tend to the flowerbed, and watch TV. We haven't had much time to enjoy our new big-screen. We need to break it in."

"I need to make more cookies. We've used a lot lately. Besides it helps me relax."

Leona nodded. "And maybe you'll find out where your kitty went." She smiled at her sister.

Betty laughed. "It was getting much too serious in there. I thought it would lighten the mood. It was all I could think of to get everyone to step back and take a breath." Betty's laughter was catching and Leona joined in.

"It worked," Leona said wiping another tear, this one forced out by laughter. "Detective Smythe got out of my face and let me breathe. I was afraid he was going to punch me or something. "

Betty got the broom and started sweeping the dish shards across the floor. "It's the advantage of being old.

You can pretend to be senile and get out of a lot of trouble that way. People usually give you anything you want to make you happy so you'll go away and leave them alone. It's like they're afraid your crazy will rub off on them." She bent over to sweep the pieces into a dust pan. "You can get pretty much anything if you know how to work people. Just don't do it front of your children or they'll throw you into a nursing home." Betty dumped the morning's disaster into the trash can.

"And it works?"

Betty winked at her. "So far."

Leona got up to get herself some coffee. "I'll have to remember that trick."

After the church services, the church group went to eat at the buffet restaurant for lunch. The waiters called them by name and visited with them whenever they came through the buffet lines. The old friends gathered at the tables in the back and listened to the previous night's events as told by Clarence. Their shocked gasps and murmurs of concern filled their corner of the restaurant.

"Don't you feel guilty?" Carly asked her with raised eyebrows. "I mean, you had something to do with that poor girl getting killed. If it were me, I'd feel awful!" She stuffed a fork full of mashed potatoes into her mouth.

Irene slammed down her fork. "Carly! What a terrible thing to say! Of course, Leona feels awful, but the murder was not her fault. Was it, Leona?"

Leona stared at the two women. She felt a little guilty about the girl dying, but surely she didn't die because she was wearing her mother's necklace. That was a coincidence. Look where she lived and who her boyfriend was. A criminal? No, Leona didn't feel guilty about what happened to the girl…not much anyway.

"Well?" Carly looked at her over the top of her glasses with raised eyebrows. Her fork had a bite of salad on it and she waved it in the air as if summoning an answer.

Leona didn't like being grilled by in-your-business Carly, but she wouldn't be satisfied until she got the answers to her questions. "No, I don't feel guilty. I wanted to talk to her about buying the necklace from her. I had the money in my purse. If she'd stuck around at the flea market, she might still be alive and I'd have my necklace." The scene from the house flashed through her mind. The pool of blood. The girl's empty stare. Her mother's necklace around that young neck.

Leona set her fork down, too queasy to continue to eat. "She didn't keep good company. I felt sorry for her. She was a pretty girl. Surely she could have done better than T-bone."

No one at the table spoke until Irene broke the silence. "Like the Bible says, bad people corrupt good manners. I'm sorry for her. I wish we could have done something to help."

Nick gave his empty plate to a waiter who came up to the table. "You should get a lawyer right away," he said, with the others nodding in agreement. "Talk to Ernie."

Betty laughed. "You'll never believe this about Ernie! He…"

"Shush!" Clarence said, "Don't gossip. We said we wouldn't say anything. Remember?"

"Oh right," Betty said, readjusting how she was sitting. "I'll just relate the facts. That's not gossip."

The ladies stretched across the table with eyes wide and eager ears. Betty whispered the plight of poor Ernie's wife. The women gasped at the anguish of Nancy and the men snickered at Ernie's new life in Mexico. All agreed that it was a shame and sat back in their seats to let the buffet quantities settle before leaving.

George softly burped, then asked, "You still need a lawyer. Anyone know of another one that might be good?"

Clarence spoke up for the first time, "We talked with

Triston Wilcox who bought Ernie's practice. He seems nice, but he's fresh out of law school. I'm not sure he has any experience with this sort of thing. He keeps saying he specializes in corporate law."

Irene spoke up. "You could use our lawyer. She's pretty good. She set up our trust and seems very knowledgeable about the laws."

Leona shook her head. "I don't need a trust. I need a defense lawyer. Anyone ever worked with one of those?"

Everyone shook their heads. "None of us has ever done anything to need a defense lawyer," Carly said as she took a dainty taste of chocolate cake. The group watched as she chewed a little, swallowed, and then said, "Church members usually don't have trouble with the law."

Leona shot Carly a look of disdain. She hadn't done anything to deserve a defense lawyer. Circumstances had thrown her into this unexplored territory. All she needed was a way out. The words were on the tip of her tongue ready to escape when Betty broke the tension.

"Perry Mason!" Betty shouted. "That's who you need. He'd get the murderer to confess in court. What I wouldn't give to see that!"

"Still looking for that kitty?" Clarence winked at Betty.

Leona snickered while the rest of the group looked at the trio in confusion. Left out of the joke, the group began to gather their things to leave.

A surprise awaited the trio when they got home. On the front porch sat Jaden, Doran, and Tiger. They waved as they saw the minivan pull into the driveway. Betty was the first one out as she hurried to gather the boys into a hug. Leona fetched the walker for Clarence before hugging the boys and inviting them in.

"Have any cookies?" Tiger asked with his hands entwined like a beggar. "We're hungry."

"What happened to all that food we brought over the day

before yesterday?" Clarence asked, wheeling up the ramp.

Jaden piped up. "We're stretching it out so it'll last longer. We wanted to try out our new shoes." He held out his foot so they could see his shoes.

Leona went to the front door and unlocked it. "How did they work?"

"Good! We ran FAST in them!" Tiger ran to the end of the porch and ran back in demonstration of his speed. "Did you see how fast I went?"

"You were a blur!" Leona said as she waved the boys inside.

"Wow! Your house is so big!" Doran said as he looked all around her living room. His eyes were wide with amazement as he viewed the neat and tidy household. He ran his hands along the sofa cushions and lightly touched the lampshade beside it.

"Thanks, but it's just a regular house," Leona said. She could see to them it was a palace. The three boys were wide-eyed as they looked at everything.

Doran seemed especially fascinated by the bookcase in the corner. He ran his hands over the spines of the books. "You got your own library," he said.

Betty called them all into the kitchen. "I might find a few things to heat up in the microwave." She motioned for the boys to sit at the table while she pulled containers out of the refrigerator. "I'm out of cookies, but I could bake some while you eat lunch." The boys heartily agreed.

Leona sat at the table with them while Betty bustled around preparing a lunch for the boys. "What brings you over here? Does your mother know where you are?"

Doran ran his arm along the tabletop, feeling the surface. "She don't care where we are right now. She's fixing to do yard work again so we thought we'd come see you."

"We like it over here," Tiger said as Leona put a glass of milk in front of him. "It's so nice and clean and big." Doran frowned at his brother and shushed him.

Leona covered her mouth with her hand lest something degrading to their mother come out in front of them. Their mother didn't deserve such good boys and it would be by the grace of God if they stayed on the right path. Their fate may be up to her and Betty and Clarence, but Miz Molly was in a better position to help them. Maybe between the four of them, they could guide them along.

Leona smiled at the boys. "We're glad you came to see us, but it's such a long ways. It must be five or six miles. Did you really run all that way?"

Jaden put down his half-empty glass of milk. "We didn't run. We jogged."

Clarence sat in the fourth chair at the table and cleared his throat. "You boys could be in the Olympics marathon someday if you keep that up." He chuckled while the boys looked at him with their milk mustaches.

"What's Lympicks?" Tiger asked. Clarence talked about it as Betty finished heating lunch and Leona poured the rest of the milk for the boys. She added milk to her shopping list.

Betty put three plates of steaming leftovers in front of the boys who picked up their forks and dove in. "No! We haven't said grace yet," she said. "Clarence, will you please do the honors?" The trio bowed their heads and he gave a short blessing for the food. When they looked up, the boys looked confused.

"Can we eat now?" asked Doran with a mouthful of food.

Leona laughed and nodded. The boys dove in again. "Don't you say grace before eating?" She put the empty leftover containers in the sink and ran water in them.

Jaden swallowed, then spoke. "No ma'am, but we're always thankful when we have something to eat." Their gratitude for the meal was evident by their smacking and MMMs of satisfaction.

Betty stirred up cookie dough while the boys ate and the

aroma of fresh baked cookies soon filled the kitchen. After they cleaned their plates, she invited them to help her put the balls of dough on the cookie sheet.

Leona picked up their empty plates to put them in the dishwasher. Seeing her open the door of the machine, Doran and Tiger ran over to watch. They wanted to help, so Leona let them put their own plates and silverware in and close the door. Their smiles and excited comments made the chore a pleasant one.

She sat down at the table as they ate the fresh-baked cookies. Leona leaned over close to Doran and broached the subject that had been weighing on her mind. "Why did you boys come here today? Is there something that we can help you with?"

Doran leaned forward, appearing to grow older as he did. "There's sumpin' we think you ought to know. That man last night. That man in the coat that was with Betty when she was talkin' to us. Who's he?"

Betty set another plate of warm cookies on the table. "You mean Detective Smythe? Tall, dark hair, suit coat?"

Doran nodded as he bit into his third cookie. "Yeah, that be him." He took his time chewing, but finally continued. "I think he's a bad man. He's at that house all the time and it ain't for a raid. He's talking with T-bone and his gang about doing jobs. We think he gets part of the money when they sell stuff."

Clarence and the ladies looked at each other, stunned with the news. They waited for the rest of the story, but Doran was too engrossed in relishing his cookie to continue.

Clarence tapped his fingers on the table to get his attention. "How do you know this?"

Doran kept chewing and started to take another bite, but thought better of it. "My uncle, Tiger's dad, he hangs around 'em sometime and I hear him talkin'. They try to get that man to do some of the jobs with 'em, but he don't want to. He says it's too dangerous for him."

"Does your uncle help him?" Clarence asked.

"Sometimes. T-bone and that man decide which houses to rob. We think they might be the ones who robbed your house."

Leona stood up so fast, she knocked her chair over. "I knew I didn't like that man!" Leona exclaimed, trying to keep the volume under control. The boys stopped chewing and looked at her with puzzled eyes. She pushed the plate of cookies closer to them, then signaled Betty and Clarence to change the topic of discussion. She smiled at the boys and picked her chair up. "Oops! I didn't mean to do that."

The boys were easily distracted. Leona didn't want them to hear what else she had to say. That conversation needed to happen later when the boys were back home. Back home on the same street as T-bone. Did she dare take them back?

Smythe likely knew these boys and where they lived. Now that he knew they were hanging around Leona, he might do something to them. What? It could be anything. But she couldn't protect them. They weren't hers to protect. Still, there had to be something she could do.

16

Leona kept a cheerful look on her face—at least she tried to—as they took the boys home before dark. She'd stopped by Miz Molly's house, but no one was home and the place was locked up tight. She couldn't leave them sitting on her front steps; it was right across the street from T-bone's house, with yellow crime tape still fluttering in the evening breeze.

At a loss to know what else to do, she drove them two blocks over to their house. Her heart was screaming at her that this was a bad idea, but no other option presented itself. It was only for one night, she told herself. Tomorrow she would go see Tristan and find out how to get those boys out of here.

Once the boys were out of the minivan and in their hovel, Leona's rage bubbled freely. "That's why this investigation keeps dragging out. He's involved with it and he's trying to cover his tracks. He knows who killed that girl and why. He wants to blame me for it so he has a fall guy. Or gal. Whatever!"

Clarence cleared his throat and uttered an agreement. "It's starting to make sense why he never wanted us around. Maybe he is a crook."

Betty played with the handle on her purse. "Maybe these boys are in danger because they know what he is and they are friends with us."

Leona gripped the wheel with a steely hand as she turned the corner to head back to her side of town. Betty's thinking had confirmed hers. Last night, Charlie had sent Smythe to talk to the boys, not realizing they were the younger brothers of one of his recruits. Charlie didn't know the predicament he'd put the boys in.

"Those boys are in danger. If Smythe found out what they told us, he'd get rid of them just like he did that girl."

"Leona!" Clarence said loudly, then lowered his voice. "Are you saying that Smythe killed that girl?"

Leona shook her head. "I don't know for sure, but it makes sense. He killed her because she was wearing something that I identified and he was afraid I would connect him to the thieves. Then his gang of thieves would unravel and he would be implicated. He would probably get sent to prison for that. No wonder he's so desperate to keep us out of the way."

"Smythe may want to pin this murder on you," Betty said. She let go of her purse handle and wrung her hands instead. "That would get him off the hook. Not only are the boys in trouble, so are you!" Her eyes were wide with fright.

"First, we have to protect those boys. They know too much for their own good," Leona said. "Maybe we should go back and get them. Their mother wouldn't miss them all that much."

"No!" Clarence said. "Smythe would call it kidnapping and that's just as bad as murder. We have to keep them safe, but we have to find another way."

"Maybe she'd agree to let us take them. Maybe we could talk to their mother when she's sober and tell her what we're doing."

Betty patted her chest, like she was trying to calm her

heart. "How long would it take to find her in her right mind? The boys said she's doing yard work."

Leona let out a loud sigh of frustration. "You're right. Maybe we should use that as a reason to take the boys out of that home." She shook her head, trying to clear the whirlwind of thoughts swirling around in chaos. "I need to talk to a lawyer or go to the mayor or something. I'm not sure. There's got to be a solution."

Leona was at Tristan's office bright and early Monday morning. Too bad Tristan and Amber weren't there. Leona went to a nearby coffee shop and got a large coffee that would surely last until they arrived. An empty cup and an hour later, Amber drove up in her old rusty sedan that had seen its better days more than a decade ago. She opened the office door, followed closely by Leona. Amber frowned when Leona asked her to turn her computer on to find out what Tristan's schedule was for the day. Was he coming in or was he in court? With the speed of a turtle and eyes rolling like marbles, she complied with the request to find out that he was coming in later.

"Then I'll wait," Leona replied and sat in one of the chairs outside his office door. She adjusted her new pantsuit jacket. Her purse always had a book in it for occasions just like this so she pulled it out and began to read.

Tristan came in about 30 minutes later looking like he'd just gotten out of bed. He carried his jacket and tie in one hand and a coffee cup in the other. His shoes appeared to be untied. *Oh brother!* Leona thought. *This man is a lawyer?* She almost got up to leave, but decided to stay because she didn't know who else to ask about her precarious situation.

She sat in the chair in front of Tristan's desk while he sorted the coffee cup from his jacket and tie before plopping into his chair. He took a sack from his coat pocket, pulled a pastry out of it, and put it on the desk in front of him. Taking a sip of coffee, he asked, "What can I do for you, Leona?" He took a big bite out of the pastry before sitting back in his chair, rocking in rhythm with his chewing.

"The police are investigating me for the murder of the girl they found in the house of the burglary gang."

Tristan stopped rocking and chewing for a moment. He leaned forward while he finished chewing, then said, "What?"

"They think I killed that girl."

He sat back and wiped his hands with a napkin. "Tell me what happened." He pushed the roll aside, suddenly intent on listening to her story. At the end, he said, "Did you kill her?"

"No! What an inane question!"

Tristan smiled. "I didn't think you did. You're not the sort. Do they have any evidence that you did it?"

"I don't think so. I didn't do it, but I think Smythe may want to make it look like I did."

He shrugged. "Then they haven't charged you."

"Not yet. Smythe is trying hard to find something on me. I'm sure of it, after the way he acted the other night. He might manufacture something to frame me for it. I don't like him." Leona leaned forward and whispered, "I have it on good authority that he's been hanging around T-bone's house before last night. Now I'm wondering if he murdered that girl."

"Who told you that?" he whispered back.

"I'd rather keep them out of this. They're just boys and have enough problems without adding killers to the mix."

"Boys? How old are they?"

Leona sat back, uncomfortable with the turn in conversation. "Not that old on the outside, but the oldest one is an old soul. He notices things and understands things beyond his years."

"How old is his outside?"

Leona shrugged. "Maybe eight or nine."

Tristan sat back as well, tapping his fingers together. "Not really credible witnesses. Is that all you got?"

"What more do you need? The kid says he's seen Smythe at that house and that he may be a part of the burglary ring. The kid lives in the neighborhood so he should know."

Tristan waved off her comment and took another bite of pastry. Leona could see his mind churning as he chewed. "So what are you saying? That you think Smythe killed the girl?"

"Maybe. I think he's a crooked cop and he should be the one who is being investigated."

Tristan's eyes grew wide. "This is a serious charge. Have you told anyone about your suspicions?"

Leona shook her head. "No one except Betty and Clarence." She thought a moment. "Oh, and Irene and George. And maybe Nick and Carly." She looked down at her hands and wrung them a little. Her mouth was getting her in trouble…again. "I might have mentioned it to everyone in the church group. I can't remember for sure. But I haven't said anything to Smythe about it."

"He's probably already heard it." Tristan sat back again and took another bite of the pastry. He chewed a little, then asked "Tell me more about this kid who told you about him."

"He's a boy that we met one day while looking for my stolen things. He, his brother, and his cousin are sweet boys and we felt sorry for them. We took food and bought them clothes and shoes. They love Betty's cookies so they sometimes walk over to our house to visit."

"And their parents are where?"

"Their mother is an alcoholic. Maybe a druggie. I'm not sure what all she is. The boys haven't mentioned their fathers. The youngest boy's father is part of T-bone's gang.

It's a terrible home they live in so we've sort of taken them under our wings. They were there, in the crowd, the night the girl was murdered. Yesterday, they told me that they'd seen Smythe at that gang house where the girl was murdered so he either knows those people or he's been working with them for some reason."

"He could have been there as part of his investigation."

"Maybe. But according to the boys, he was there before our burglary."

"Doesn't prove a thing. He's probably investigating other burglaries. Maybe he suspects the gang that lives there is committing the crimes. It makes sense."

"But I get the feeling that he's not the good cop like people think he is."

Tristan shook his head. He ate the last of his pastry and wiped his hands off as he chewed.

Leona made an effort not to roll her eyes. She squirmed in her chair while he was finishing his breakfast. His rocking and chewing were making it hard for her to keep her tongue in check. Someone should teach him office and client manners.

Making a last big swallow, Tristan threw away the napkin. "You can't file a complaint based on feelings. We need concrete evidence or testimony."

"So you're telling me to forget about it?"

"Unless you have something more than just feelings and a young boy's word, I recommend it. Chalk it up to personality conflicts and leave it alone. The truth will come out in the investigations."

"Not when a crook is doing the investigation."

"Then bring me hard credible evidence."

Leona looked at her hands as her shoulders slumped. Now what? She didn't trust Smythe, but no one believed her gut feelings were right. She dared not get Doran any closer to danger than he already was. If Tristan didn't believe her, likely no one else would either.

Tristan wiped the pastry crumbs from his shirt onto the floor. "Why don't you do this. Write everything down: dates, times, people, places. Document your suspicions. Then we'll take a look at what you have and determine if you have enough evidence to file a complaint of police misconduct. They will require no less."

Leona wiped her slacks off, mindlessly emulating Tristan. "But he'll know who reported him."

Tristan agreed. "That's part of the process. He has the right to defend himself against his accusers."

"I'm not comfortable with that." Leona shifted in her seat as if pushing away from an unpleasant situation. "Maybe I shouldn't say anything."

Tristan leaned across the desk and looked intently at Leona. "It's your civic duty to report corruption. If something's going on that's illegal, we need to put a stop to it. But," Tristan wagged his finger at her, "if he's innocent, he could cause quite a stir about your credibility. Falsely accusing a police officer is no small thing. You have to be absolutely certain of what you're doing."

Leona sighed as she closed her eyes and rubbed her forehead. Should she take that kind of risk? What if she was wrong? Smythe didn't seem like the kind of man who would forgive and walk away. He'd figure out that the boys were tattling on him. Would they be in danger of revenge?

At the same time, the boys were sure Smythe was the one around the gang house so something was going on. Surely the police chief and the mayor would want to know. But how could she be sure whether he was checking on burglaries or was part of the gang? She rubbed her temples as the stress of the decision weighed heavier on her.

Tristan rattled some papers, signaling he was a busy man. "You don't have to decide this minute. Think about it for a day or two. And I feel I must remind you again, I'm not a criminal case lawyer. I specialize in—"

"I know. I know. Corporate law." Leona straightened

her jacket. "I'll write things down so I can see what I have. I'll come back later and talk to you about it."

17

Leona stopped by the car wash on her way home. The shower for her car would help her own desire to wash away all that had happened. She sat back in her seat as the machines pulled her car through the water and soap. She wished they could wash away all the worry she's had lately. She felt unclean, having had some role in the murder of a young woman. The need for a shower overwhelmed her. Once again, she prayed for forgiveness.

As she vacuumed the car out, several items clanked their way up the hose. She hoped it wasn't the hearing aid Clarence lost several months ago. It was probably rocks from his shoes or loose change he'd dropped when he bought drinks for everyone at the Sonic.

The clean minivan lifted her spirits as she drove to the grocery store to pick up a few things. When she came out of the store, she nearly dropped her bags when she saw Smythe leaning up against her car talking on the cell phone while two police officers leaned against their cars blocking hers in the parking lot. Torn between going back into the store to wait for him to leave and confronting him, she gave in to the latter.

"Why are you here?" she called out angrily as she

walked up to the minivan. She stomped her foot.

He quickly hung up his cell phone. "We need to search your minivan. Do you mind?"

"Yes, I do," she said. "What are you looking for? Got a warrant?"

He heaved an impatient sigh. "I was hoping you'd cooperate. I'm looking for clues to a murder."

"In my minivan? I didn't kill that girl."

"Then you won't mind if I look."

Leona almost threw down her sack of groceries in anger, but she remembered the jar of pickled okra that was too expensive to break. She set the bags down gently on the ground by the minivan. She wasn't comfortable with them searching her vehicle, but maybe they'd see that there was nothing in there to bring suspicion on her. She nodded slightly and unlocked the doors.

Smythe looked in the front of the minivan first while the two officers raised the back door to look in that compartment. One lifted the backseats out of the floor while the other let a drug-sniffing dog out of the police car. The dog jumped into the back of the minivan and sniffed around. He came out and went in the side door, sniffing all around. Leona held her hands up to protest, but put them back down when she realized she couldn't do anything about the dog hair. She hated it. She'd have to go back to the car wash to vacuum it out again.

She watched Smythe search the front seat and glove box. Oddly, he didn't seem to look all that hard there. He looked in the backseat where Clarence usually sat. He ran his hand up under the seat. He seemed confused and searched there more vigorously. He stood outside the car with his hands on his hips, then repeated his efforts around Clarence's seat. She heard a low growl in his throat.

He walked to the back to talk with the other officers in low tones. The three of them walked the dog back to the car where they continued to talk. After a short conference, the two police officers got into their cars and drove way, leaving the minivan free to move.

Smythe came back toward Leona. "Okay, you're free to go," he said with clinched teeth. He slammed the minivan rear door with a vengeance of a frustrated man.

Leona cried out as the door slammed. Her fists were clenched as she fought to control her anger. She stomped her foot with rage. "Just what did you think you'd find?"

He pressed his lips together and looked away. Turning back to her, he growled, "We had a tip that there were drugs in your car."

For a moment, Leona was stunned into silence. "That's ridiculous! Utterly ridiculous! Why don't you go search your friend, T-bone's car? Bang his car door off its hinges! Have you questioned him? He's probably the one who killed that girl. I know you hang around with him. Maybe you're the one who's hiding something. Maybe you need to confess your sins." She looked down at her index finger pointed at his chest and wondered how it got there.

His dark glasses hid his eyes, but couldn't hide the fiery glare that came at her. "How do you know that?"

Leona felt empowered. "Little eyes have seen you there more than once. Is T-bone a friend? Are you protecting him by trying to frame me for the murder? Or maybe you're the guilty one."

He whipped the glasses off his face so that she got a good look at the hatred in his eyes. She saw it clearer as he closed in on her face. She could smell his breakfast on his breath and cringed, pulling back slightly. "Prove it!" he spat at her. He stood there a moment, letting his message sink in. He put on this glasses, got into his car, and drove away.

Leona stood by her minivan, staring at Smythe's taillights as they lit up at the stop sign before turning the corner. Her hands shook slightly as she regained her composure. She pushed the button to open the back of the minivan. Setting her groceries in the back, she muttered to herself, "Wow, I guess I got under his skin."

Leona hauled the last bag of groceries into the kitchen just as the phone rang. She yelled for Betty to answer it, but when she heard no response, she got it herself.

"Hello. I'm not interested in contributing to your cause or buying anything."

Silence followed. Leona was about to hang up when she heard a weak voice. "Miz Leona?"

"Who is this?"

"This is Miz Molly."

"Oh!" Leona sat down at the table and put the phone on speaker. "So nice of you to call."

"Miz Leona, are Doran, Jaden, or Tiger at your house?"

"Why no. I haven't seen them today. Why do you ask?"

"Their mom is over here wondering where they're at. She hasn't seen 'em since yesterday." She paused, then whispered into the phone. "But you know that don't mean much."

"Yesterday! And she's just now looking for them?" Leona's heart started beating faster. It was a long ways between the two houses. They could be anywhere. "Do you have any idea what route they'd take if they were coming over here?"

Miz Molly let out a long sigh. "I don't know. They'd take shortcuts so could be alleys or streets or anywhere."

Thoughts swirled in Leona's mind. Were they near home? Were they almost here? Were they in between? Most of all, were they okay? Those young boys should never be out on the streets like that. What to do? What to do?

"Miz Molly, have you looked all over the neighborhood there?"

"We've looked a little, but found nothing. Since they've gone to your house the past couple days, we were hoping they wandered over yonder again."

"Why don't you look around there more thoroughly and I'll drive between here and there looking for them. Between the two of us, surely we'll find them."

"Okay. I'll call you if they turn up."

"Thanks, Miz Molly, I'll bring them home if I find them."

Leona didn't take the time to look for Betty and Clarence. Leaving a quick note telling them where she'd gone, she left in her minivan and traveled toward the north side of town. She took alleys and streets that went past parks to look for the boys. Several times, she thought of different routes so she turned around and explored those as well.

At a red light, she closed her eyes and rubbed her temples like she always did when anxiety took over. She didn't want to quit looking for the boys, but she didn't know where else to look.

A honk from the car behind let her know that the light was green. She had no alternative but to face the boys' mother. She would be furious again and the language out of her mouth would hurt Leona's ears. It was no less than she deserved. She should have sent those boys home with harsh words the first time they showed up. She'd rewarded their wandering behavior with new clothes, shoes, and food. Her charitable heart had encouraged the boys to continue their long walks through town.

She drove up in front of Miz Molly's house in time to see Kendra come dashing out of the house toward the minivan. Leona tried to see if there was a smile or a frown on her face. She hit the side of the minivan as Leona turned the motor off and got out.

"We can't find 'em." Kendra was huffing and puffing. "Me and Zilo just got back from running all over, hollering at 'em to come home."

Miz Molly came outside and waved at Leona to come in. Kendra put her arm around Leona and walked beside her to the steps.

All of the children she'd met on the north side of town seemed to want to touch her and hug her. Leona wondered what kind of attraction she was to them. Maybe it was nothing more than knowing that she might buy things for them. Or could it be something deeper, more basic? Love itself? She loved children which is why she taught elementary school for so many years. Since she'd retired, she missed being with children. She gave Kendra a warm squeeze as she walked up the steps into the house.

As she walked up, she saw Lila being held back by the strong arm of Miz Molly. Her brow was furrowed with anger and her mouth was covered by Miz Molly's hand. Miz Molly wasn't letting her speak the words.

Miz Molly yelled at Lila, "This is MY house and it's a Christian home. No profanity is allowed in here. So if you wanna say something, it better be clean or I'll throw your good-for-nothing backside outta here. You understand?"

Leona stayed on the front step in case she needed to escape. Miz Molly seemed to be in control as she turned to look at Leona. "Didn't find 'em?"

Leona shook her head. "I looked everywhere I could think of and nothing." She squeezed her eyes together to hold back the gathering tears. "I'm sorry. I should have never gotten this routine started, where they come over to my house whenever they take a mind to."

Lila tried to push Miz Molly's arm aside, but couldn't do much against the strength of the larger woman. "You trying to take my boys away from me? I won't let you! They're mine!"

"Settle down, Lila!" Miz Molly pushed the woman back a step. "Your boys have wandered all over town since the day they was born. If they wandered off today, it's nothing but your own doing. If you was sober and a real mother to them, they'd stay home like they oughtta. Miz Leona didn't have a thing in the world to do with it."

"She buys them things to draw them away from me!" Lila looked at Leona with hatred and fire in her eyes. Her hand was clenched like a claw, threatening to tear into Leona's skin. Miz Molly pushed Lila back another step.

Leona took a step back and got ready to run as fast as her old legs would go. The bloodshot eyes of the angry woman conveyed her lack of emotional or physical control. The clawed hand reached in her direction and waved in the air.

Leona fought her fear and tried to stay calm. "I'm not trying to pull them away from you. I didn't invite them to come over. They came of their own accord." Leona waved her hands in the air. "It doesn't really matter right this moment. We need to concentrate on finding them."

Miz Molly agreed just as Kendra came running in the door, nearly knocking Leona down. "Grandma! Miz Maria saw the police take the boys away. She said they was over in the park and a police car stopped and talked to them. The policeman chased them. She said Doran fought him and told Jaden and Tiger to run, but they didn't get away. The policeman chased them and caught them and took them all away."

Leona's heart froze. Smythe. He had the boys. She'd caused this. She put her hand over her mouth to keep a cry of distress from escaping. Doran must have known they were in trouble, if he told his brothers to run. Leona could hardly breathe. She began to wobble as Miz Molly came to her and helped her into the house.

Miz Molly told Kendra to get a glass of water for Leona. She looked at it before drinking. She could only hope that it was clean, but her head spun so much that she needed the water more than she cared about germs. She thanked the boy for bringing it to her and sipped it. The tepid water did little to calm her nerves.

Lila still stood ready to take on Leona. "This is your fault!"

Leona wailed through the growing stream of tears. "I'm so sorry. I never ever meant to get those boys involved in my search for Joe's ring. I never intended any harm to anyone." She wiped her eyes. "Don't worry. I'll get my lawyer on it and we'll have them out in very short order." She took another sip of water, then gave the glass back to Zilo.

Lila stood with her fists clenched. "You got a lawyer?"

"Yes, and he'll get them out."

Miz Molly sat beside Leona. "Lila, you go on home. Miz Leona will make sure your boys get home. She cares for them as much as you and I do. Now go on."

Lila shuffled her feet as if they were arguing with each other over staying or going. She pointed her shaking finger at Leona. "You get my boys out of jail and never come back. You hear me? Stay away from them!" Her jaw worked with profanities, but one look from Miz Molly helped her keep them unsaid. She stomped out the door, slamming it behind her.

Leona's heart was about to jump out of her chest. Lila had frightened her so much that she felt faint. If it hadn't been for Miz Molly's strong presence, she might have fainted from fear and anguish over the boys. She dropped her head in her hands.

"She's right. It's all my fault."

"You said you'd call your lawyer to get 'em out."

Tristan. She had to call Tristan. Her dizziness subsided with the call to action. She'd call Tristan to get right on it. She looked around for her purse, but it was nowhere to be seen. Miz Molly sent Zilo out to the minivan to see if it was there. Soon he came bouncing in with her purse over his shoulder. Hunting through the bag, she found her cell phone and dialed Tristan's number.

Leona drove in the garage next to the Newport soon after her call to Tristan. The house was quiet when she entered. Betty was nowhere to be seen. Puzzled, she looked around for a note from her sister explaining where she'd gone. As she headed for the living room, the phone rang.

"Leona, this is Tristan," came the voice on the phone. "I called the police station and found out they picked up three boys who were wandering the neighborhood around your house. They were put into juvie hall on the suspicion of burglarizing homes. They were the ages you indicated so I'm wondering if they could be your three helpers that they picked up."

Leona's voice got stuck. Not Doran, Jaden, and Tiger! Who on earth would think those sweet boys could do something like that. She sucked in her breath. What had she said to Smythe when he searched her car? Something about little eyes watching him?

"Tristan," she yelled into the phone, "it's a lie! I just got back from Miz Molly's and a lady in that neighborhood saw the police pick them up over there."

"Are you sure?"

"Absolutely sure! Something's not right. Go to the police station and find out what's going on. Those boys are NOT thieves! It's Smythe! He thinks they'll rat him out and they'll point the finger at him for his associations with T-bone. He's the one who murdered that girl! She gave him away by wearing my necklace."

"Calm down, Leona! You're letting your imagination run away with you."

"Either do what I say or I'll do it myself! Go down there and check on those boys! Oh my, oh my. What they must be going through." Leona paced around the kitchen with the phone to her ear. "We've got to help those boys."

Tristan was silent for a moment. When he spoke, his voice was calming. "I'll go check on them and call you back as soon as I know something."

"They'll need a lawyer so you're it. Don't let one of those cheap public ones do the job. You represent them and I'll pay their fees."

"Leona, I keep telling you. I'm not a criminal—"

"You are now! Go and see about those boys!"

"Oh, here you are!" Leona had run across the street looking for Clarence when she couldn't find Betty at home. The two of them stood in his living room, staring at her after she interrupted their work. Betty held a large garbage sack and Clarence was in his chair with a lap full of magazines. "What are you doing?"

"I'm helping him clean his house," Betty said looking surprised that anyone would ask.

She looked around at the myriad of magazines and newspapers stacked around the room. "Yes, I see. We don't have time for that now. Come on! The boys have been hauled to juvenile hall because they were walking over here to see us. Tristan thinks they'll be charged with burglarizing people's houses. I think Smythe is doing it to them to get to us. You know what else he did? He searched my minivan! Imagine my embarrassment at having my vehicle ransacked by that…that…"

"Scofflaw?" Clarence looked pleased with himself for being the nearby thesaurus.

Leona stared at him for an instant, wondering where he'd learned that word. "Yes, that scofflaw! We have to go help those boys."

Betty put down her garbage sack and went to Leona. "Did you call Tristan? He might be able to help."

Leona nodded. "He said he'd check into it and call me back."

"You should go back to the house and wait for his call. He'll know what to do better than you storming down there to demand answers." Betty looked at Clarence who nodded in agreement. "He might be calling right now."

"Stay here if you want," she told the cleaning pair, "I'm going to the rescue."

"You three again?" The desk sergeant threw down the papers he was carrying. Leaning forward across the counter, he said, "I told you before! We're working on it. Now go home and leave me alone!"

Leona slammed her purse down. "Don't get curt with me, mister! You've arrested three boys—three innocent boys—and I want them released. I'll be responsible for them. I'll pay their bail or whatever you need to let them go."

"I don't know who you're talking about. What boys?"

Betty stepped up beside Leona and opened her purse. She pulled out a little bag full of cookies and held them out to the sergeant. "Their names are Doran, Jaden, and Tiger. They're cute as buttons!"

The sergeant looked at the ladies and at the cookies. He rubbed his forehead, then pushed the cookies back toward Betty. "Are you bribing me for information about an arrest? That's a crime, you know."

Betty tittered. "Bribe? Of course not. You look hungry and I happen to have these going to waste in my purse. Wouldn't you like one or two or five?"

The sergeant balked, but the cookie temptation was strong and he gave in. He gently lifted one of the cookies out of the bag, barely holding it with his fingertips. He took a nibble from it and a look of deliciousness flashed across his face. He quickly masked his opinion and finished the cookie in record time.

"It might be that those boys were arrested by Detective Smythe. He said they robbed your house."

"No, they didn't!" the trio said in unison. Leona shouted it too loudly for the small room, drawing the attention of several other officers behind the counter and people on their side of the counter. She lowered her voice, "I'm sure of it. Smythe wants them off the street because they can place him at the scene of the murder."

Shaking his head as he reached for another cookie, the sergeant told her, "He found the evidence on them. They had a string of pearls that you reported missing. He caught them red-handed." He bit into the cookie with relish. "They're guilty all right."

Betty's hand went to her chest as she gasped. "My pearls? They had my pearls?"

The sergeant shrugged as he bit into another cookie. He signaled for them to wait there while he went into the back.

The trio huddled together. "Smythe framed them," Leona said. "I'm sure of it. I let it slip that they were watching him and now he's trying to take them out of the picture."

Betty shook her head. "But they had my pearls. How could they have gotten them if they didn't get them from the house?"

"Betty, dear," Clarence said as he squeaked forward to stand beside her, "If Leona is right, Smythe may have had them and slipped them to the boys when he arrested them. They're too innocent to understand what entrapment is."

"That's it!" Leona exclaimed. "He entrapped them. Tristan can use that to get them out. I need to call him." She dug in her purse. "Where's that cell phone now that I need it!"

As she was rummaging, the sergeant returned with a manila envelope. He opened the end and slid the contents out on the countertop. A small string of pearls bounced across. Betty let out a soft cry of surprise and picked them up.

"These are mine!"

"There you have it, folks," the sergeant said with fanfare. "Evidence. Smythe found these on the boys. Can't fight evidence. They're guilty all right."

"No, they're not!" Leona shouted. "They were framed!

Smythe planted the pearls on them!" Leona pounded the counter in frustration.

Betty pulled the bag of cookies toward her, but the sergeant reached out and grabbed another cookie before Betty put them away. He looked at Leona sternly before saying, "Not that again! Look, lady, I've been as nice as I can be to you for as long as I can. This crazy idea of yours about our Detective Smythe has to stop. Maybe you're losing your mind and getting senile or something, but Smythe would never do something like that. He's one of the good guys!"

"And you protect your own, even to the detriment of innocent children." She picked up her purse.

"You're nuts, lady!" The desk sergeant stuffed the pearls back into the manila envelope. "That man has been through a lot during the past year. His wife died of cancer last year. Did you know that?"

Leona felt a stab in the heart. Anyone losing a spouse, even an enemy, had her sympathy. She missed Joe badly and Detective Smythe likely missed his wife as much as she missed her Joe. She felt a twinge of guilt for being so nasty to him, but it passed quickly and anger returned in its place.

The desk sergeant went on. "Her cancer meds cost over $20,000 a month. He sold everything he could to raise the money. He remortgaged their house. We all pitched in to help as much as we could. But, she didn't make it and he's been left with all those bills. Don't you think he's been through enough heartache without having an overbearing old woman harass him?"

Betty sniffed. Clarence cleared his throat but said nothing. Leona got mad.

"No sob story is going to make me change my mind. Those boys had nothing to do with burglarizing our house. I want to see them! They'll tell me the truth. Where are they? I want to talk to them."

The desk sergeant sat down in his short chair and bit into his cookie. "Are you a parent or a guardian?"

"No. I'm the overbearing old woman who they are supposed to have robbed. I deserve to see my thieves."

"It doesn't work that way. They're minors. Unless you're a parent or a guardian or their lawyer, you can't see them."

Leona wasn't sure what to do next. She could pound on the desk and demand to be taken to see them. She could ask for the police chief and complain about the poor quality of service. She could even start saying "here kitty kitty" in hopes he'd think she was crazy and let her have anything she wanted. She threw out the last option because she was afraid they'd take her to a rubber room.

Clarence took her elbow. "Let's go talk to Tristan. Maybe he can get in and see them."

Leona stood firm, afraid to lose her last toehold on getting the boys out herself. If she left, everything was gone.

Betty took her other elbow. "Let's go, sis. There's nothing more you can do. Let Tristan take it from here. He'll know what to do."

Unable to fight against it, she jerked her elbows away from them and stomped her foot. Facing the sergeant, she said firmly, "You tell Smythe that I'm onto him and he better not hurt those boys. I'm as sorry as I can be about his wife, but my focus in on the wellbeing of those boys. I can cause him a lot of trouble and I will do it if so much as a hair on their heads is out of place. You tell him that for me."

She let out a grunt. "Come on, gang. Let's get out of this sorry place." She spun on her heels and stormed out.

18

"Don't tell me to calm down!" Leona paced in the living room of her home. Tristan sat on the edge of one of the new recliners, watching the meltdown of the elderly woman. Occasionally she would stop, sit down, and think. The frustration didn't let her sit there long. She would let out a cry of aggravation and begin pacing again. The new carpet padded her angry stomping. Betty and Clarence sat on the sofa, watching her wear a pace pattern in the carpet while Tristan held his peace to see what would happen.

After ten minutes of watching her sister, Betty laughed out loud. Leona stopped to stare at her and the two men. Betty laughed again. "Remember," she said, hardly able to speak for laughing, "remember when Daddy said you had the worst temper he'd ever seen? That one day you would stomp a hole in the ground and fall in?" Betty kept laughing while the others looked on unamused. "I can hear him now. 'Leona, quit your stomping around! You're going to break your foot.' He would have loved to see you stomping around now." She reached for a tissue and wiped her eyes.

Leona put her hands on her hips and stomped her foot. Her face reddened by lack of control of the action, she said,

"Betty! This is not funny! Those boys are being set up as the fall guys for Smythe. I don't know how deeply he's involved, but my gut tells me he's behind all of this!" She stomped her foot again and Betty started laughing harder.

Tristan stood up and tried to stop Leona's pacing. She shook him off and continued to pace while wringing her hands.

Tristan sighed and put his hands on his hips. "There's no evidence to what you're saying. You could be wrong—"

"I'm not wrong!" Leona stopped and glared at the young lawyer.

Tristan held his hands up in surrender and sat back down on the edge of the recliner. "I can't—no lawyer could go forward from here without something to go on. The law doesn't recognize your gut feeling as something that will hold up in court. There's nothing else I can do."

Leona tsked him as she paced. "Perry Mason would have found a way. So would Matlock."

Tristan closed his eyes and pinched the bridge of his nose as he crinkled his face. "Those are TV shows. Fictional stories written by people. If anyone suspects you don't know the difference, the boys will be the least of your worries."

Silence and stillness filled the room while Leona stopped to stare at the guest intruder in the place where Joe's recliner once sat. Was he implying she was crazy? How dare he! She put her hands on her hips and gave him a glare that made molten lava seem icy. Tristan squirmed uncomfortably under the intense heat.

Betty cooled the tension. "I bet you didn't figure on getting into this kind of mess when you bought Ernie's practice, did you, Tristan." She smiled at him and gave a soft chuckle.

Tristan stared at her for a moment before one side of his mouth rose a little. "No, I thought I was buying a nice quiet practice where most of my clients would want help with their businesses or the city might want a lawyer on retainer. I'm not prepared for criminal law."

"Well, you better get prepared for it, buster!" Leona barked before she started pacing again. "Three boys are depending on you to set things straight." She stopped pacing, slowly realizing the futility of her anger. Alienating the only lawyer she trusted at this point in time would be detrimental in her goal of helping the boys. The heat of her ire dissipated. She moved to stand in front of him and said softly, "I'm depending on you to set things straight. Please."

A look of resignation came across Tristan's face which released itself through a heavy sigh. "I've got contacts that might be able to help me. A friend from college went into criminal law. Maybe he can help me out."

"Good!" Betty cried with glee. "Everything's settled! By the way, Tristan, you should watch those lawyer shows and get some ideas on how to be a good lawyer. You can expand your skills and Leona will quit wearing a hole in the new carpet. Now then," she clapped her hands together, "how about some cake all around?" She jumped up from the sofa and scurried into the kitchen. The sound of water running was quickly followed by the smell of coffee signaling that she was getting cake for everyone.

Tristan stood and said loudly, "I really need to be going. I have a lot of homework to do."

Betty came running out of the kitchen and grabbed him. "No! I've already cut you a piece of cake so you have to stay and eat it." She pushed him back toward the recliner. "Sit. I'll have it out in no time." Away she scurried back to the kitchen.

Clarence cleared his throat. "No use fighting these two girls. You won't win." He gave Tristan a wink and a grin. "Trust me. I know. Even Joe knew it was no use resisting once they got an idea in their head."

Tristan returned a half smile. "I'm discovering that." He

twiddled his fingers a few turns and then asked, "So, Leona, your dad really said you had the worst temper he'd ever seen?" Leona's glare turned his cheeks red and he looked down at his hands that twiddled faster.

Betty's chortle rang from the kitchen. "Tell him the story, sister!" The rattle of silverware could be heard on the tray they used to serve company.

Leona hated telling the story, but she knew Betty would tell it if she didn't. Betty loved to embellish the family tale to the point that little truth remained in it. Leona sat in her recliner and sighed. "I've always had a temper."

Betty's giggle of concurrence drifted into the living room.

"I can't help it, I was born that way." Leona paused to see if Betty had anything to add. Hearing nothing, she went on. "When I was young, I picked up some foul language at Daddy's feed store and tended to use it when I was mad about something. Mom would haul me off and wash my mouth out with soap."

Tristan's eyebrows shot up. "Literally wash your mouth out?"

"Of course. Parents didn't allow language like that in those days. Mom held my head over the sink and pushed a bar of soap into my mouth. It tasted awful and I would gag and scream. But she kept it in there until I said I wouldn't talk like that anymore. Of course, she told Daddy and he punished me on the other end."

Tristan gasped. "He hit you?"

Leona frowned. "Spanked! He spanked me. Hard. Across my backside. And don't look at me that way. It wasn't child abuse. It was what I deserved for disobeying the rules of the family. Cursing wasn't allowed. I knew it and I did it anyway. I suffered the consequences of not minding my parents. If a few more parents disciplined their children, we wouldn't have such a mess in our schools and—"

Betty came in the room, carrying the tray with cake on it. "Here it is! Chocolate cake!" Clarence leaned forward from the sofa and cleared the few magazines off of the coffee table. Betty set the tray down and hurried back to the kitchen to bring back the cups of coffee for everyone. Leona passed out the plates of cake.

Tristan took a bite of cake and smiled. "Wow, this is really good cake, Betty!" He took another one before sipping the steaming coffee. "I love old fashioned hospitality!"

Clarence laughed. "It always involves good food. No one can beat a southern cook."

Betty beamed. "Thank you, boys. I love cooking! Leona, I believe you were saying—" She lifted her fork in salute to her sister. "Your mouth washings—"

Leona put her fork down. "It went on for several years. Me getting mad and spouting off. Mom dragging me to the sink for a mouth washing. I couldn't help it. I was releasing my anger. It went on until one day, my dad sat me down and said, 'Leona, this can't go on. I'm tired of spanking you and we're using up all the good soap in your mouth. We got to figure out another way for you to express yourself without saying bad words.' So together we decided that instead of spouting out something I wasn't supposed to say, I'd stomp my foot. He knew I would get mad about things and needed an outlet. So I started stomping and he quit buying so much soap. End of story." She got a big piece of cake on her fork and stuffed it in her mouth.

Clarence chuckled and shook his head. "I always love hearing that story."

19

Leona put the last of the supper dishes in the dishwasher and closed the door. Wiping off the counters, she thought of what her next steps would be. First, she needed to find a way to get those boys out of where they were, but then what? They couldn't—or shouldn't—go back home. Her stomach hurt to think about them living in that firetrap of a house with a mother who, deep down, probably cared for them, but was otherwise worthless. Where else could they go? Foster care? The three brothers would likely be split up and that would be traumatic for them. Doran mothered his brothers and seemed to have done a good job at it.

She stood still, lost in thought, scrubbing the same place on the countertop over and over again. The boys were doomed to a life of hardship unless she could find a way to get them out. They were good boys and deserved so much better. Her shoulders slumped under the weight of her concern.

She rinsed out her dishrag and picked up the last of the things in the kitchen. Today's newspaper had been tossed on the cabinet, unread so far. The day had been too busy for that. She picked it up and headed to her recliner in the living room to read it. She needed to relax and get her mind off her problems.

Walking into the living room, the sight on the sofa stopped her in her tracks. Her mouth fell open as she saw watched Clarence and Betty sitting close. Too close. Clarence's hand brushed Betty's knee and Betty giggled. Not her usual giggle, but a schoolgirl giggle. Leona blinked her eyes, not wanting to believe what she was seeing. When she heard the word 'kissie-poo,' she spun around and rushed toward her office in the back room.

She plopped into her desk chair. Putting her elbows on the desk, she covered her face in her hands. *Is the world going mad? Innocent boys in jail. Bad cops. Incompetent lawyer. Betty and Clarence—I don't even want to think about it!* She took her hands off her face and entwined them together. She said a prayer.

After a quiet time spilling her requests to God, she felt better. Joe's lamp sat in the middle of the desk. When she turned it on, the bright light made her squint her eyes. After her eyes adjusted, she opened the newspaper and tried to focus on the stories. The usual items were there: city council bickering, street repairs, crime in the streets. She turned to the comic section, hoping for a chuckle.

In an instant, her ears were overwhelmed by the deafening sound of glass and other things breaking and exploding. She heard Betty let out a hoarse scream. Clarence yelled out something she couldn't understand. The noise seemed to go on forever, but died away soon after the squealing of tires reached her ears. After that, only the sound of dogs barking broke the eerie quiet.

Leona grasped her chest to keep her heart from pounding its way out. She yelled out Betty's name as she ran down the hallway toward the living room, but got no response. Running through the kitchen and into the living room, the sight nearly made her faint. Her picture window was gone. The shredded curtains moved in the breeze. Her new TV screen was blown to bits, with only the shell of it still on the entertainment center. Glass was everywhere, large pieces, pointed shards, and slivers glittered across her carpet in the lights from the kitchen. The walls were full of holes. The air smelled of smoke.

On the floor, Betty lay with her eyes closed. Blood ran down her face. Her sleeve was turning red. Clarence was slumped over on the sofa. His blood dripped down onto the upholstery.

A cry of alarm escaped her throat without her bidding it. She knelt beside Betty and felt her neck. A soft beating pulsed under her hand, eliciting a sigh of relief. She stroked Betty's hair softly and whispered that everything would be all right.

Someone pounded on the door, yelling to be let in. Leona recognized the voice and rushed to the door to open it. A neighbor, a middle-aged man in his pajamas, came in and stood gaping at the scene.

"Jason, call 911! Hurry! They're hurt!" Leona screamed out as she rushed back to Betty. A sob escaped her lips, followed by a guttural scream.

"I already have," Jason said as he rushed to her side. "I'll check Clarence. He looks bad!" As he moved to the sofa, the faint sound of a siren drifted in through the shattered window

Leona couldn't force any more words through her tears. Leona lifted Betty's reddening sleeve. Blood oozed out of a hole in her skin, repulsing Leona, but she looked away for something to stop the bleeding. A box of tissues lay nearby so she grabbed a handful and placed it over the wound to stop the bleeding and to hide it from her eyes. The siren was getting closer and Leona felt relief that help was coming. She swallowed the lump in her throat and managed to say, "How's Clarence?"

Jason shook his head. "I don't know. He's been hit several places and his pulse is very faint."

A wail erupted from Leona. "Who could do this to us?

We're haven't done anything!" She sucked in her breath as she thought about Smythe. She shook her head. He might be a bad cop, but even she didn't believe he would be capable of something like this. It must have been T-bone and his thugs. They were the kind who'd shoot at innocent people to shut them up. Red strobe lights flashed around the room, making her more dizzy and lightheaded than before. At the same time, she was relieved. Help was here.

Leona sat in a waiting room, staring at the floor, her mind down the hallway where Betty was getting care. Clarence had already been wheeled into surgery. She'd called his son Tom and Betty's daughter Diane, and both were on their way there. She'd called her daughter Jennifer who was also on the way. She made one more call to Irene who would spread the word to the church group. At this point in time, all she could do was wait and pray.

Wait and pray. She'd waited and prayed in this same room while they worked on Joe two years ago. He'd collapsed at home clutching his chest. The EMTs had come and rushed him to the hospital. All she could do then was wait and pray. When the doctor finally came to see her, his face told her the story. No words were needed to tell her Joe was gone. She dreaded seeing the doctor again. Afraid of what his face would hold. Afraid of losing her sister. Afraid of being alone.

She hated the hospital because it reminded her of so much sadness. The smell of cleaner, the sounds of nurses and people going by, and the loudspeakers asking for help in other departments. They all made her uncomfortable. She didn't want to sit in the chairs or on the sofa. Who knew who'd been there last and what germs they had?

She paced up and down until she was too tired to walk any more. She sat on the edge of a chair, afraid to lean back in it too far. Her pants and blouse were stained by Betty's blood. She needed a shower and her soft warm bed.

Irene and George were the first to arrive, followed shortly by Darren, May, Nick, and Carly. Their casual dress told of the hurried rush to the hospital. When everyone was there, they had a group prayer, after which they began to circle around her like flies around a picnic. Carly led the group in demanding details of what happened.

They offered her coffee, food, hugs, words of encouragement. She only faintly heard their conversations because her own thoughts were so loud. The questions tumbled in her mind like clothes in a dryer, round and round, tumbling over and over. Why, why, why... Who would do this, who would do this, who would do this... It should have been me, it should have been me, it should have been me...

A firm hand on her shoulder brought her out of her turmoil. She looked up into the worried face of Tristan. "Who told you?"

"George called me. I wanted to let you know that I'm here for you."

"Thanks." Her eyes were watery so she avoided looking at him. She put her hand over his and squeezed. "I should have listened to you."

Tristan leaned over the back of the chair and shoulder-hugged her. "I've spoken to the police. They have theories on who did this, but not enough evidence to bring charges yet. That will depend on Betty and Clarence."

"Depend on them? Do they have to formally press charges?"

Tristan stood up and backed away. All eyes were on him and he seemed nervous. "No," he said protractedly. "I mean the police don't know yet what kind of charges they'll file against whoever did this." He looked around with raised eyebrows, as if willing the others to read his mind so he didn't have to say the words. "You know, assault or—or— maybe something more serious."

Carly let out a loud gasp. "Or murder!" she cried out

before her wails echoed around the room. Nick quickly put his hand over her mouth and loudly whispered, "Get a hold of yourself!" in her ear.

Irene quickly went to Leona and put her arms around her. "Now, Leona, don't worry, dear. I'm sure they'll both be fine and we'll be laughing about this before you know it." She patted Leona and turned to glare at Tristan. "Don't you know what Leona has been through tonight? She's very delicate right now."

Leona wasn't shocked. The thought had crossed her mind while waiting. She gently pushed Irene away from her. "I've already thought about that possibility. If Smythe investigates, it will go nowhere. Can we get someone else, an impartial investigator to look into it?"

Tristan cracked a slight smile. "You get your wish. Detective Charlie Walters does homicides and assaults."

Leona let out a sigh of relief. "First good news of the day."

A scrub-clad young man sauntered in the door. "Mrs. Templeton?" He scanned the crowd that had gathered. Fingers pointed at Leona in the chair. "Are you Mrs. Drummond's sister? She's asking for you."

Leona stared back at him, looking for any hint of his next words. His face held no darkness and his voice held no bad news. "Is she going to be all right?" Her heart felt a small glimmer of hope.

The young man smiled. "Yes, she's fine. She has some bruises and a lot of cuts that should heal. A bullet went through her upper arm, but it missed the bone. It did little damage. A few weeks rest and she'll be good as new. She's a very lucky lady."

A flood of tears threatened to break lose, but Leona blinked them back. She patted her chest as she allowed herself to breathe again. Praise the Lord! Betty would live! Sounds of joy and prayers of thanks filled the room until someone asked, "How's Clarence?"

It came suddenly. The dark cloud covered the young man's face, and Leona knew his next words would be terrible. She felt her chest tighten again, preventing her from taking another breath.

"I can't divulge his condition except to next of kin," he said. "But I will say this, he needs your prayers."

20

"Leona?"

The sound came from nowhere, yet was everywhere. It called to her, but she didn't have the strength or will to answer it.

"Leona. Wake up."

As her unsettling dream faded, Leona stirred and wondered why her back and neck hurt so much. She reached to rub her neck and realized she was sitting in a chair. Blinking her eyes open, she looked into the face of Betty who was in the hospital bed next to her. She jumped out of the chair, but the dizziness made her drop back into the seat. She grabbed the arms of the chair to steady herself.

"Should I call the nurse?" Betty asked as she reached out toward Leona.

"No, I just stood up too fast." Leona stood again, slowly and carefully, hanging on to the sides of the bed. "I'm fine. How are you feeling? You have a little more color in your face."

"I feel weak. I hurt all over, like I've been run over by a truck." Betty moved her arms around until Leona took them gently and held them still.

"Don't move around! You don't want to pull this IV out of your hand." Leona smoothed the tubes to make sure they weren't pulling on the needle in Betty's hand and that she was getting all the oxygen she was supposed get. She clasped the hand without the IV in it and held on to the cold fingers, trying to warm them with hers.

Tears welled in Betty's eyes. "What happened? I can't remember. I just remember noise. Loud noises and falling off the sofa. I don't understand." A tear slid down the side of her face and into her ear.

A tear fell from Leona and landed on the bed beside Betty. "It's all my fault. Mine alone. I should never have drug you and Clarence into the crazy search for Joe's ring. Smythe was right. We got into things that we had no business being around. And now you and Clarence are hurt—"

The door swung open as a cheerful young nurse came in. "I see you're awake. Good! Let's take some vitals and see how you're feeling." She proceeded to punch the buttons on the monitor and gather information. "How are you feeling?"

Leona gave Betty a tissue. "Pretty sore," Betty said after wiping her eyes.

"Do you want a little pain medication?"

Betty shook her head. "No, it makes me crazy. I just want some aspirin so I can go home to recover in my own bed. My sister can take care of me."

The nurse smiled. "I think you'll be able to go home today, but the final word comes from the doctor. He'll be in later." She finished her vital-statistics gathering and asked before leaving, "Need anything?"

Betty nodded. "I need to know how my friend Clarence Brown is doing. Can you tell us?" A look of concern flashed across the nurse's face as she came back to the bedside.

"He's not on this floor so I don't know much about it. All I know is he could sure use your prayers." She patted Betty's arm softly and gave Leona a weak smile. "Need anything else?"

Betty grabbed the nurse's arm before she could pull away. "Why can't you tell us? He's been our best friend since we were little. He's all alone in town and needs us."

"I'm sorry, the privacy laws don't allow us to discuss medical issues with anyone not designated by the patient. You're not on his list."

Betty huffed. "Trust me, Clarence wouldn't mind if we knew about him."

The nurse shook her head and pulled her hand away from Betty. "Sorry, I can't say."

"What if we promise we won't tell where we heard about his condition? Just tell us how bad it is."

The lifting of her eyebrows and her shrug told the sisters that the nurse wouldn't reveal any more information. "Can I get you anything?" she asked again.

"Just a straight answer, but since you won't give it to me, no, I don't need anything."

The nurse smiled. "Your breakfast should be here soon. Maybe that will make you feel better." She breezed out the door to check on other patients.

Betty slammed her hand on the bed. "I don't like this, Leona! Clarence is our best friend. We ought to go sit by his bed until Tom gets here."

"I know, but there's not much we can do." Leona clasped Betty's hand. "They won't tell us anything. The doctor just says he needs our prayers. So let's say a prayer, shall we?"

Betty snorted. "Pray while you go around to every room in this place and find him!"

"I don't want to leave you! When Diane comes to sit with you, I'll go looking. She should be here soon."

Betty sat up straight in bed and started pulling at the

tubes stuck around her. "Diane won't be here until this afternoon. If you're not going to go now, then I will!"

Leona restrained her and pushed her back onto her pillow. "Okay, I'll go!" Leona smoothed the tubes back down and looked to see that Betty wasn't bleeding anywhere. "You are so stubborn when you've a mind to."

Betty lay there with a gotcha look on her face. "Don't be too long. I need to know how my honey's doing. And comb your hair before you leave. You look—" She skewed her face with her opinion.

Leona opened her mouth to ask for more details, but thought better of it. She found a small comb in her purse to comply with Betty's request. After checking herself in the mirror, she left to go find Clarence.

Leona found Tom in the ICU waiting room talking with the doctor. Tom looked up and motioned for her to join them. She sat down next to him, took his hand, and squeezed it.

Leona," Tom said, "the doctor is telling me that Dad's pretty bad." He looked at the doctor and told him to continue.

"Clarence suffered a bullet wound in his right chest. It grazed his lung, but mostly missed everything critical. He has cuts and puncture wounds from the shattering glass and bruises from falling."

Leona's hand moved to her mouth to stop a sob from exiting. Tears streamed down her cheeks. She checked her sleeves for tissues, but found none. Tom pulled out his handkerchief and handed it to her.

The doctor took off his glasses and stared at Leona. "Are you one of the ladies that was there when the shooting occurred?" He waved his glasses toward her bloodied slacks. Leona nodded. "Have you been checked out?"

"No." She wiped her nose with Tom's handkerchief and took a deep breath to control her weeping. "I'm okay. I wasn't in the room when it happened."

With a tone of voice that lay bare why he became a doctor, he said, "You should get a doctor to check you over. The trauma might have affected you more than you know." His hand covered hers and she felt his caring and concern.

"Thanks, Doctor. I'll do that in the next few days." She looked at Tom, then back at the doctor. "Last night, our neighbor said he'd been shot several times and you say only once."

"I suppose to the untrained eye, some of the puncture wounds looked like bullet wounds. We've done the x-rays and I can assure you that he was only shot once. It took a while to get all the glass shards out. Some of them were really deep, but fortunately they missed the critical places as well. He was a lucky man."

The vision of the bullet-riddled wall flashed before her eyes. "By the Grace of God, he is." Tom uttered an amen to her prayer.

The doctor looked at his tablet. "In addition to his wounds, he suffered a heart attack which is why he's in ICU. We don't think it was a massive one, but it did some damage on the right side of his heart. He's stable, so we need to go in and put a stent in to increase blood flow through his heart. There's some risk with his condition weakened by his injuries, but I feel he's strong enough to withstand it. It's something that needs to be done as soon as possible. But we need your permission to do the procedure."

"Sure, Doc, do whatever you think best." Tom looked at Leona who nodded her concurrence. Not that he needed it, but maybe he needed confirmation that he was doing the right thing.

The doctor spent a moment typing on his tablet before rising to leave. "The paperwork is started and things are set up. A nurse will be back shortly with papers to sign. We're scheduled to take him down later this morning." He cracked a small smile and left in his usual rush.

Tom exhaled a big sigh and ran his hands through his thinning, brown hair. He needed a shave, but she doubted he'd get one very soon. Leona put her arms around his faded-sweatshirt shoulders and gave him a hug. She'd known this man since he was a baby across the street. He'd grown up so fast. Here he was now, making life-and-death decisions about his elderly father. Time passed so quickly where their children were concerned.

"What happened, Leona," Tom said through his hands on his face. "How did Dad end up being shot at your house?"

Leona took her turn at running her hands through her hair. *I must look a fright, she thought. I haven't showered or fixed my hair since yesterday. Yesterday, before the nightmare started. I want to turn back the hands of time. I'd leave the investigation to Detective Smythe.*

"Leona?" Tom looked impatient.

She sat back in the uncomfortable chair. "I'm not sure. We've been looking for the people who robbed our house. Apparently we stepped on some toes somewhere or scared the thieves. Things got out of hand."

"Where were the police? Aren't they investigating the robbery?"

"Well, yes and no. You see, we think the detective is behind all the robberies in town and we felt—I felt I had to do it myself."

Tom's eyebrows shot up. "What? You, Betty, and Dad have been doing police work?"

Leona held up her hands. "I know you think that's crazy, but it's not. Plainly, something devious is going on. We felt it was our civic duty to expose police corruption. We had to do it ourselves because we had nowhere else to turn."

Tom shook his head in disbelief as his face reddened. He stood and paced around, mumbling something to himself.

Leona wrung her hands. "We had no idea it would go this far. I'm so sorry."

A nurse came with a folder full of release forms for Tom to sign. Leona left while Tom tended to the duties at hand. She didn't feel like facing his wrath. Clarence would have to find another chauffeur because she was certain Tom wouldn't allow her to take him anywhere again.

Diane stood up. Her frown lines were deep and many as she stared at Leona coming into the room. Her years of tanning had given her an older-than-her-years look. Her black leggings under a too-big sweatshirt and long graying hair added to her unkempt appearance.

"What have you done to my mother!" The accusation left no room for answering the question so Leona stood a safe distance away near the doorway.

"Did you find Clarence?" Betty asked, peering around her outraged daughter who was standing with her hands on her hips. "Did you find anything out?"

Leona nodded, but kept her eyes on the human pit bull. Diane had always been this way, even as a young girl. Headstrong and obstinate, she never let go of a wrong done against her. She took after her dad in that respect, the opposite end of the spectrum from her mother. "He's in ICU because he had a mild heart attack. They'll put a stent in place later today. He has a bullet wound, but it's not serious. Tom's here so he's with him."

Diane spun around to face Betty. "That does it! You're coming home with me, Mother. It's obvious Aunt Leona can't take care of you. I'll do it and keep you safe from whatever thugs you're mixed up with thanks to Aunt Leona. You're too old to be running around and chasing criminals or whatever. I don't know what either of you was thinking."

"Now, Diane—" Leona reached out toward the pit bull in a peace gesture.

"Don't 'now, Diane' me!" the pit bull spat back at her. She pointed her finger at Leona and stabbed the air in her direction. "I've already called Jennifer. She's on her way to see about getting you settled in a facility that will watch you and keep you out of trouble."

Leona stopped dead in her tracks, blindsided by the remark. Aghast, she tried to say something, but words refused to leave her mouth. Instead, she shut her mouth and returned the burning glare back to the pit bull. What little control she had over her anger prevented her from doing anything else. She didn't want to hurt Betty by telling her niece just what she was thinking.

"Diane, go get me a soda from the machine down the hall." Betty said quietly. When Diane refused to break the stare down with Leona, Betty became more insistent. "You heard me, young lady. I want a soda and I want it now. Please."

Without breaking the gaze, she replied to her mother, "I'll be right back." She sidled around Leona like she was a leper before leaving the room.

Betty reached out to Leona. "How is Clarence? Will he live?"

Leona was still livid at being challenged by this whippersnapper of a niece. She made her way to Betty's bedside while seething. Betty reached out to take her hand and shook it so hard that Leona's upper arm flapped. "Answer my question! Will he live?"

As if coming out of a trance, Leona tried to focus on Betty's earnest face. The emotion there helped Leona push her anger away enough to respond. "It sounds like he will be fine. He's cut up like you and a bullet hit him in the upper right chest, but didn't hit anything major. And he had puncture wounds like you do. The biggest concern is his heart. The doctor said they'd put in a stent to get the blood flowing again. But not to worry. They think he'll be fine in time."

Betty's hand went to her heart. "Oh thank you, Lord!" She wiped her eyes with the edge of the sheet. "I was so afraid I'd lost him just when I found him."

An unsolicited smile found its place on Leona's face. Finally! Something not about the shooting. Since she brought it up, I might as well ask. "What's going on with you two? I saw you flirting with each other on the sofa right before the shooting. Don't tell me that you—and he!" Leona put her hands on her eyes. "Seeing you two, it hurt my eyes. It doesn't seem right."

Betty chuckled softly. "We weren't doing anything wrong. Even I'm surprised at how I feel! During this whole thing with the robbery, I started looking at him in a different light. He's a very kind and caring person, and he's lonely. You know I love you, Leona, and I appreciate how you and Joe took me in after Vince died, but you don't need me. You can take care of yourself just fine. As much as I love living with you, I miss having someone to take care of. I need to be needed and Clarence makes me feel needed. That sounds crazy, I know, but I need someone that can't take care of himself."

"Clarence fits that bill." Leona sat on the edge of the bed and took her sister's hand. "I don't know what I'd have done without you after Joe died. I know you're a caretaker and Clarence will need one when he gets home. He'll be glad he has you around to help." The sisters hugged until the pit bull returned with Detective Charlie Walters behind her.

21

Leona hung up the telephone in the kitchen. Drawing a deep breath as she searched for courage, she went to face her daughter in the living room. "That was the insurance adjuster. He's not too happy with me."

The disgust in Jennifer's eyes halted Leona in her tracks. "Tell him to take a number and get in line," she growled.

Jennifer stood in front of her mother with her hands on her hips, looking just like Betty's pit bull. Tall and thin like her father, she wore jeans and a stylish shirt that made her look younger than her 50 years. She tapped her foot in impatience just like Leona used to do.

I used to be that thin, Leona thought. *That girl better be careful or she'll end up pleasingly plump like me.* Leona almost laughed out loud, thinking of how their roles had been reversed.

Jennifer gestured at the plywood that covered the picture window and waved her hand toward the bullet holes in the wall. "What happened here, Mom? What have you been doing that would get your house shot up?"

"I didn't do anything," repeating the words Leona had heard so often during Jennifer's teenage years. "I'm not the one who shot the house up." Suddenly feeling very tired,

Leona settled into her recliner and put the footrest up.

"Diane says you dragged her mother and Clarence into the seedy parts of town looking for Dad's ring. She said you'd been asking questions and stirring things up with some sort of criminals. Criminals with guns! I want to know what's going on!"

Leona rubbed her forehead to soothe her brain aches. "Our house was robbed. I told you about that."

"Yes, and I thought everything was settled. The insurance paid for the things that were stolen and put your house back together. Wasn't that enough?"

"No, not for me. I wanted your father's ring back."

"Is that when this whole mess started? While you were chasing Dad's ring?"

Leona nodded. "The police didn't seem like they were trying very hard and I wanted my things back. This police detective—Smythe's his name—kept trying to put me off, but I've found out things about him. He's involved in some way with the thief who robbed our house—T-bone's his name—so that means that Smythe may be a member of the burglary ring and not really a good guy. I think he had a hand in the burglary. Or at least covered it up."

"Did you tell the other police officers about that?" Leona bobbled her head in response. Jennifer shook her head in exasperation. "Is that a yes or a no?"

Leona shifted in her chair, uncomfortable with defending herself to her daughter. Her daughter that should be more respectful. "I reported things to the front desk sergeant, but he didn't take me seriously. In fact, the sergeant defended Smythe. So I knew they wouldn't listen to me until I had evidence so I was trying to find some."

"You're not a detective, Mom! Let the police handle it."

Leona slammed her hand down on the arm of her chair. "I can't! Something's going on around here and I think they should investigate the investigator."

"What proof do you have? Has your 'investigation'

turned up some deep, dark secret that the police don't know about?"

"I told you. We found some things out about Detective Smythe. I have three little witnesses that say they've seen him associating with felons." Leona drew in a quick breath. "The boys! I've forgotten about the boys!" She jumped out of her chair and pushed Jennifer to the side. "I've got to find out if the boys are okay. I need to call Tristan and see if he knows anything. Then I need to call Miz Molly because she's worried about them too." Leona hurried to the kitchen and dialed Tristan's number.

"Who are you calling, Mom?" Jennifer stood behind Leona.

"My lawyer. He knows where the boys are. He can go check on them."

"What boys are you talking about, Mom? Does Mr. Lanyard know about these boys?" Jennifer looked confused and worried.

Amber's voice came over the phone and Leona asked to speak to Tristan. While she waited, she explained to Jennifer. "Ernie Lanyard ran off with his secretary so a young lawyer, Tristan Wilcox, took over his practice. He's been working with me on—Hello, Tristan? This is Leona. Hey, I need you to do me a favor. Could you go to juvenile hall again and check on those boys? Please? And get back to me as soon as you can. I'm worried about them."

After a short discussion, Leona hung up and turned to talk to Jennifer. Jennifer had Leona's purse and was rummaging through it. "What are you doing? Stay out of my purse!" Leona grabbed for it, but Jennifer pulled it back out of her reach.

"I'm convinced Diane was right. You're losing it. So I'm taking your car keys. I don't want you running off and getting into trouble again."

Leona lunged at her purse again, but Jennifer sidestepped and held the purse behind her. Leona growled lowly. Another attempt for her purse fell short as well.

Anger erupted from Leona like a volcano. "How dare you tell me what to do! I am your mother! I raised you to know better than to treat me like this!" She moved toward Jennifer trying to reach her purse.

Jennifer moved away and held the purse out of Leona's reach. "I want you to stay out of trouble until I can figure out what to do with you. I think the time's come for you to move near me so I can keep an eye on you. There's a new independent living facility in town that I think you'd like. Brett and I have been talking about it for a while and we think it's time."

"You and your brother are talking about me?" Leona clenched and unclenched her fists. "I'm perfectly fine here in my own home. I don't need to be put away somewhere, waiting to die. I'll wait to die right here."

Jennifer's expression softened a little. "Mom, aren't you ready to have someone take care of you for a change? They'll cook for you and clean your apartment once a week. Doesn't that sound nice? And they have lots of activities where you can socialize with your friends. It'll be great. You'll love it. You'll see."

Jennifer's pleading eyes infuriated Leona. Her children wanted to take her home away from her and stick her away in a strange place. Out of sight and out of mind. "No. No. And I won't go."

That response changed the pleading eyes to ones that mirrored Leona's fury. "You can either go peacefully or by force. Either way, Brett and I have already decided it." Jennifer lifted Leona's keys to her minivan out of her purse and rung them like a bell. "In the meantime, you stay home and start packing." She stuck the keys in her pocket and tossed the purse back to Leona.

After Jennifer left to go check into a hotel, Leona paced all over the house, seething with rage. Her children were holding her hostage in her own home. How dare they! She slammed a towel on the bathroom countertop and stared at herself in the mirror. The veins on her neck were throbbing with her angry heartbeat. She was startled by the sight. I need to calm down or I'm going to give myself a stroke. Then they'll really have an excuse to stash me away in a home somewhere.

Going to her recliner in the living room, she plopped down like a cow too tired to go any farther. She rubbed her temples and quoted a Bible verse: Overcome evil with good. She felt a little release of tension. Overcome evil with good. It helped. She kept repeating the verse, trying to release the pent up stress caused by the shooting and Jennifer.

The phone rang, jolting her out of her trance. She held onto her chest to calm her pounding heart. She tried to catch her breath before lifting the phone from its recharge station beside the chair.

"Hello?" She was still out of breath.

"Leona? Is that you? Were you running?" Tristan's voice sounded genuinely worried.

"No, I'm fine. What's going on?"

"I thought you'd like to know that the boys are being moved to another facility."

"What? Why? Who's doing this?"

"Smythe."

Leona's heart started racing again. "No! He can't do that!"

"He filed papers that the boys are troublemakers and they are being sent to juvie in the next county."

"He's trying to keep them away from me because he knows that they know me and they'll tell me the truth. You've got to stop him!"

"I talked Charlie into investigating Smythe's finances. I just talked to him and he said things look suspicious. They haven't completed their investigation yet so it's too early to draw any conclusions. But you may right about him being connected with the burglary ring. Those boys might be able to put the finger on him."

"When are they being moved?"

"Any time now, if he hasn't already."

"Tristan, you go talk to Charlie or a judge and get him to stop the transfer. I'm on my way down there to stop him if I can. Those boys might be in danger!"

"Let me handle this, Leona—"

"No time to talk. See you downtown!"

Leona hung up the phone and dashed into the kitchen where her purse still sat on the table. Grabbing it, she hurried to Joe's workbench in the garage. She dumped a coffee can of nuts, bolts, and various other metal items on the workbench and pawed through the pile. Pushing the screws and bolts around she found what she was looking for. The spare key to the Newport.

Once inside the car, she rummaged through her purse to find the cell phone. Her hands shook as she punched the buttons to find her calling list. The chore seemed to take too long as her fingers seemed determined to hit the wrong buttons. She let out a "Heaven help me!" and a moment later, she found the right number. She punched it and prayed he was home. He was. "George, I have a job for the church group."

22

Leona pulled around to the side of the police station and parked the gunboat of a car, thankful for making it in the ancient car. When the Newport started in the garage after sitting for so long, she'd said a prayer of thanks before pulling out. The old car didn't drive as nicely as her minivan. *Why was Joe so crazy about this car?* she wondered. *No wonder he drove it instead of me. He probably thought I couldn't handle it.*

She quickly got out and hurried toward the back of the police station where she knew the main jail was. As she rounded the corner of the building, she saw Smythe pushing the boys into the back of his car.

"Smythe!" Leona yelled. "You leave those boys alone. Put them back!"

Smythe jerked around, his mouth agape in surprise. A snarl quickly formed there as he pushed Tiger inside the car.

"Help us, Miz Leona!" Jaden cried out. Smythe pushed his head down and forced him into the backseat with his brothers before slamming the door shut.

"Get out of here, you old bitty!" Smythe growled at her. "I'm tired of your ugly face!" He opened his car door and got in. The engine roared to life as Leona ran up beside the car.

"Stop!" As the car began to move, she cried out louder, "Help, police!" She tried to open the door. "Citizen's arrest!" The car sped up, twirling her as it left her behind. She stumbled around while trying to catch her balance as she spun. Falling and breaking a hip wouldn't help save those boys. Finally regaining her equilibrium again, she weaved a crooked path back to the Newport, her arms splayed out like a balancing pole of an acrobat. She got into the giant car and found her cell phone. Thankful for a redial button, she quickly called George. "He's in a black Queen Victoria! He's headed toward the north side of town. Don't let him get past the city limits!"

George didn't respond at first. "You mean, a Crown Victoria? Did it say Ford on the front grill?"

"I don't know!" she yelled into the phone. "I just saw the word Victoria. It's a big black car. Don't let it leave town!" She threw the phone on the bench seat beside her, then started her car. When she threw it into gear, the powerful motor pressed her back in the seat. The tires squealed in protest at the sharp turn out of the parking lot in pursuit of Smythe.

She soon caught up with Smythe on Main Street, heading out of town. *He's not speeding because he's trying not to attract attention to himself. He doesn't want to answer a bunch of questions from the cops. I don't think he knows this car so maybe if I get in front of him, I can make him stop.*

Pulling out from behind him, she eased the Newport into the other lane and pulled up beside him. He glanced over to see who was passing. His eyes widened in surprise when he saw Leona shaking her fist at him and motioning for him to pull over. He quickly turned right at the next corner, leaving Leona driving on Main Street.

She sped up and pulled into the other lane before

sliding the Newport around the next corner. The black Ford went past the intersection ahead. She floored the accelerator to reach the intersection quickly, then stomped on the brakes. The Newport leaned heavily on two wheels to make the corner onto Adams Street. With a whomp, it settled back down on all four tires before speeding down the street again. The black Ford was nowhere in sight. Heading down Adams Street, she caught a glimpse of taillights on a black car on her left as she went through an intersection. Smythe was going back to Main Street.

Leona turned the Newport gunboat at the next corner and headed back toward Main Street. Taking a quick look to see if traffic was coming, she didn't stop as she turned onto Main Street. The black car was a block ahead of her. She pushed the Newport until it came up beside the black Ford.

Without taking her eyes off the road, she poked the armrest, trying to find the button that would roll down the window so she could yell at him. Realizing the old car had crank windows, she let out a cry of frustration.

Looking over at him, she saw Smythe talking on his radio. No doubt he was calling her in for troublemaking. The boys were in the backseat, yelling and waving at her. The fear on their faces made her want to cry. She motioned for them to get down.

She looked ahead in time to see a car coming her way, head-on. She quickly braked and pulled back on her side of the double yellow lines. The car went by with its horn blaring. She deserved it. Her heart pounded wildly as she let Smythe pull ahead. Someone was going to get hurt, if she didn't watch out. Plus the police had been alerted to her tailing Smythe. She pulled into an empty parking spot and called George again. "He's headed north on Main Street, just past Sixth."

"We've got him. Don't worry. He won't get far."

Leona watched Smythe as he moved down Main Street.

Suddenly, he took a turn back toward Adams Street. After he turned, Leona could see a red Chevy pickup and a white Cadillac Escalade driving slowly side by side on Main Street. It was Nick's truck and Carly's Escalade! They had forced Smythe to turn back toward Adams Street. Leona left her parking spot, and headed toward Adams.

A police car pulled up behind Leona without its lights on. She glanced at her speedometer. They couldn't stop her for speeding. She was only going 35 miles per hour. Turning on her blinker, she turned on Adams. Up ahead, the black Ford was moving slowly, allowing her to catch up. She followed at a safe distance and stayed in her lane, giving no reason for the police to pull her over.

In the rearview mirror, Leona saw the Escalade and Chevy truck behind the police car. The caravan continued down the street until Smythe turned back toward Main Street. Leona and the police officer turned on their blinkers and followed him back to Main Street.

The edge of town is not far off. He doesn't have far to go before leaving town. Now what? I can't let him out on the open highway. The city cop behind me will have no jurisdiction after he crossed the city limits. He'll take off and I'll never see those boys again!

Back on Main Street, the line of cars slowed almost to a crawl. Leona craned her neck to see around the black Ford. Easing her car closer to the yellow line, she could see cars driving very slowly, blocking traffic on Main Street. Although she couldn't be sure, a truck straddled the white line, blocking both lanes. And the truck looked a lot like George's and Irene's Chevy truck.

Leona laughed out loud. The church group had come to the rescue! They were keeping Smythe in town until Tristan got matters settled at the court house.

She watched Smythe veer into a small side street. Leona and the police car followed him around the corner. Smythe's brake lights came on and he stopped in the middle of the street. Leona saw George's red truck across the street with boxes strewn all the way across the road like they had fallen off his truck. He had his back turned to Smythe's car, but she could tell he was talking on his phone.

Before Leona could decide what to do, Smythe's car stopped in the middle of the street. Smythe tried to go around the back of the truck. She saw the Escalade and Chevy pickup pull up alongside the boxes in the street, blocking his way.

Seeing the black Ford's backup lights come on, Leona pulled her behemoth car crossways across the street as well. Smythe was hemmed in. The lights on the police car flashed on as she pulled into position. At last! The police knew what Smythe was trying to do. Tristan had finally worked it all out and now Smythe would be arrested. The boys were safe, thanks to the church group. A smile came across her face and she breathed a sigh of relief.

The policemen jumped out and stayed behind their doors with guns drawn. "Get out of the vehicle! Keep your hands where we can see them."

Leona looked at Smythe's car to see if he was going to comply with the instructions. No movement. He sat as still as a statue. He'd been caught red-handed. Surely he had the good sense to know when he was beaten and give up. She could see no movement. Not even in the backseat. The boys have done what she signaled and were huddled on the floor of the car.

Leona heard the policeman yell again. "Get out of your vehicle! Keep your hands in sight!" Smythe remained frozen in place in his car. She wanted to go over there and pull the man out. Shame on him for taking those boys!

The door of Leona's car was flung open and a policeman was there with his gun pointed at Leona. "Get out! Keep your hands where I can see them!"

Leona let out a squeal of fright, then said, "ME?" She

waved frantically at Smythe's car. "I'm not the criminal! He is!"

"GET OUT OF THE CAR!" The policeman stared down his arm, across his pistol, and into Leona's eyes. "Now," he said through gritted teeth.

Leona recognized Don Janus, but she'd never seen him with fury in his eyes. The look scared her. She put her hands up and stepped gingerly out of the car. The policeman swung her around so she faced the car, but the motion made her dizzy. She staggered and started to fall. The cop reached out and steadied her so that she kept her balance.

The radio on his collar buzzed, blending in with the buzzing in her head. She couldn't make out what the message said, but she understood when Janus told her, "Wait here." He left her hanging on to the car door as he moved with his gun drawn around the Newport and toward Smythe's car. His partner Officer Torrez came from behind Leona to join him.

"Smythe, get out of the car, sir!" Officer Janus stood with his gun held in both hands pointed at the driver's seat. Leona could see Smythe staring straight ahead, gripping the steering wheel. "Sir, get out and keep your hands where I can see them."

Smythe drooped his head. He pulled out a gun and held it against his head.

"Don't do it, Smythe! Don't do it!" the cop yelled through the window.

Seeing the gun, Leona rushed around her car and came up behind the cops. "Not in front of the boys! Please! Not in front of the boys!" Her impassioned plea rang through the air around them all. "They've seen too many bad things in their short lives. Don't make it one more."

For a long moment, time stood still as everyone watched the man with the gun to his head. Then ever so slowly, the gun began to move down. When it was no longer visible, breath came back to Leona. Officer Torrez opened the back door of Smythe's car and the three boys came spilling out. They jumped up and ran to Leona, wrapping themselves around her while she moved them away from the big black car.

23

Leona stood on the front porch of her home while she waved good-bye to Jennifer. Once the car was out of sight, Leona let out a yell of freedom and went inside.

"You seem happy." Betty was sitting on the sofa with her crocheting, smiling at Leona. The new picture window let in plenty of light for Betty to see what she was working on.

"I love my daughter, but she's too bossy for me to enjoy for very long." Leona sat in her recliner and picked up the newspaper, pulling up the footrest. She thought about turning on her new 65-inch flat screen TV, but thought better of it. She took a sip of coffee before settling in to read the paper. "There's an article about Smythe on the front page of the paper today."

"Yes, I know. I read it. I feel very sorry for him."

Leona put the paper down. "Because of him, you nearly got killed, not to mention Clarence and his heart attack."

Betty shook her head without looking up from her crocheting. "But he was trapped. He helped the burglary ring so he could pay for his wife's cancer medicine. He couldn't afford it otherwise. He did it for love, not personal gain."

"Why didn't he stop after his wife died?"

"T-bone wouldn't let him. He probably threatened to expose him, or kill him, or whatever other unpleasant things he could think of. Smythe wanted out, but knew he'd lose everything if he left. He was trapped."

"He kidnapped the boys! He was taking them to who knows where so they'd be out of the picture."

"T-bone threatened them. Smythe was moving them to keep them safe from him."

Leona grumbled as she unfolded the paper. "Doesn't matter. He doesn't deserve any sympathy. Whatever's happened to him, he brought it on himself." Leona let out a snort of contempt and went back to the paper. She read the article for herself and as hard as she tried to fight it, she came to the same conclusion as Betty. In some ways, he was a victim too, although Leona didn't want to admit it easily. Her anger at him for threatening the boys had not eased in the week since he took them.

"Don't be bitter, dear. Everything turned out in the end. T-bone admitted to killing his girlfriend. He and his gang are in jail. Smythe is off the police force. The boys are back home with their mother." She looked up from her crocheting. "Well, maybe not everything."

The phone rang and Betty put down her crocheting to answer it. Leona went to get the coffee pot to refill both their cups. A shout of delight drew her back into the living room. Betty told her, "Clarence is coming home tomorrow!" The smile on her face lit up the room as she talked on the phone.

Leona smiled back at her. "Tell him we'll come get him in the minivan and deliver him safely to his home." She returned to the kitchen to let Betty have some privacy. She cut the corner off a pan of brownies and popped the piece in her mouth. Its rich flavor and sweetness filled her whole spirit and she closed her eyes. Chocolate! Her own personal nirvana drug.

"Leona!" Betty broke the chocolate spell. "He's coming home!" Betty giggled like a schoolgirl. "He's coming home!" she sang as she danced around the kitchen.

Leona leaned against the cabinet. "Are you saying that you're in love with him?"

Betty stopped and stared at her sister, then started dancing again. "I guess I am! Ha ha! I guess I am!" She broke out in a crazy love-stricken laugh that frightened Leona a little.

"Has he proposed?"

Betty rubbed her finger along the countertop. "No, not exactly. But I expect he will. He's been looking for a wife for several years now. He's a lonely man, you know."

Leona nodded. Since her last refusal of his advances, he'd turned his attention to Betty. Just as well. Betty was a caretaker and needed someone as badly as Clarence did.

"I guess life will change for all of us. I'll have to get used to living alone."

Betty was quiet for a moment. Her face slowly transformed to a worried look. "That will be hard on you. You'll be all alone for the first time for the first time in your life."

Leona shrugged. In all of her decades of life, she'd never lived alone. She went straight from her parents' home into her home with Joe. Could she live alone? The house would seem very empty with only her in it.

Betty broke into her thoughts. "We could all live together in one house. It would be cheaper for all of us that way."

Leona shrugged. "Let's cross that bridge when we get to it."

"Here we are!" Betty let out an excited yell as the trio pulled into Clarence's driveway. Tom pulled his car up to the curb. Leona got Clarence's walker out of the back of the minivan and brought it around. Betty and Tom had

Clarence out of the minivan. She stood back out of the fussing and let the other two guide and encourage Clarence toward his front door.

George and Irene stood on the porch, welcoming the group home and holding the front door open as Clarence made his way through. The living room was tidied up and clean. The piles of magazines were still there, but were neatly stacked and dusted. The kitchen sparkled. Casseroles with written heating instructions filled the refrigerator. The house hadn't been this clean since Barbara died.

Leona stood on the front step and wondered whether she should go inside. Tom had spoken fierce words to her about endangering the old man's life. Guilt still weighed on Leona about that night. All she could do in response was apologize. When Tom finished his well-rehearsed tirade against her, he seemed to feel better and they parted on amiable terms. Still, she knew she was not well thought of.

So this is how it's probably going to be, she thought. *Betty would be devoted to Clarence and at his house all the time. She doesn't need me anymore. And Clarence won't need me anymore either. But what about me? Do I need them? Can I live by myself after all these years?*

She got his bag and accoutrements from the hospital out of the minivan and took them into the house. Clarence was sitting in his recliner while Betty flittered around him, making sure he had his remotes and anything else within reach. Leona set the bags down, then took his big-lidded cup into the kitchen to get him some water.

"Thank you for everything, Leona," Clarence said from his chair. "And George and Irene, God bless you all. You did a lot of work to get this place to look this good. I guess it was a mess."

"Yes, it was," Irene offered before George came up behind her to nudge her into silence.

"It was a group effort," George said. "We'll go and leave you to get settled." They bid all good-bye and left.

Tom came out of the back bedroom and got the bags. "Thanks for bringing him home, Leona. I think he's more comfortable in your minivan than in my sports car and he can get in and out of it much easier."

"You're welcome. I'm always happy to give him rides." She turned to go. "How long will you be here?"

Tom shrugged. "Through the end of the week, then I need to get back to work."

"If I don't see you again, have a safe trip home. Clarence, if you need anything, you've got my number."

"I'll be home in a bit," said Betty as she stood behind the recliner.

As Leona turned to leave, Clarence yelled out, "Wait!" He struggled to get out of his chair. "I want you to be here for this!"

Tom pushed his father back into the recliner. "Dad, what do you need? Just tell me what you want and I'll get it for you."

Clarence let out an exasperated groan. "It's not something you can help me with." He held his hand out toward Betty. "Come here, sweetheart," he said in a singsong voice. "I wanted to get down on one knee to say this, but Sonny boy here won't let me out of this chair."

Eyebrows couldn't have gone any higher nor mouths opened any further as everyone watched Clarence take Betty's hand and say, "I love you, Betty, and I'm asking you to be my wife. Let's spend the rest of our golden years together. What do you say?"

Betty giggled. "You don't need to be on one knee to say that. I love you too, Clarence, and would love to be your bride." She leaned down and kissed him.

Tom frowned. "What?"

Clarence smiled. "My sweetheart."

Betty beamed. "My darling."

Leona stared. "My word!"

Leona pulled her minivan into her garage. Her insides felt heavy with sadness. She hated change. That's why she and Joe had lived in the same house for 52 years in the same town they'd both been born and raised in. She'd had trouble adjusting to having Betty around when she first came after Vince died. Watching Clarence propose to her made her realize that now she didn't want her to leave.

Opening the door to the house, emptiness came out and engulfed her. Her shoes clacked on the tile floor, echoing through the empty house. Her life was that way, especially without Joe. Empty. Meaningless. Lonely.

She didn't know what to do with herself. She went to the bedroom and sat on the bed. Opening the nightstand drawer, she pulled out the dark silver pistol she'd purchased after her visit at the pawnshop. It felt heavy in her hands. She marveled at how pretty it looked. She put it up in front of her opened mouth and pulled the trigger. A line of water shot out of the end into her mouth. A couple of good pumps gave her a nice swallow of water. She wrinkled her nose. The water was stale. She'd have to change it more often for drinking, but for now, the flower pots around the house could use a good watering.

She danced around the house, acting foolishly and shooting her houseplants with the water gun. She laughed out loud. The pawnshop owner told her to get a gun and she had: a water gun. It looked like the real thing, so maybe it would scare someone off. But she'd never have to make the decision of whether to shoot someone or not.

She aimed at her zeezee plant in the corner of the living room. Taking careful aim, she pulled the trigger. The stream from the gun reached out maybe four feet, almost reaching the plant. She took a step closer and tried again, this time hit her target.

Damp lines on the carpet showed her improving aim. As she emptied her gun on her English ivy plant, she decided that maybe being alone wasn't so bad after all. In fact, it might be fun. She let out a laugh at herself.

Her cell phone rang, drawing her away from her childish play at watering her house plants. She got it on the third ring. "Hello?"

"Mrs. Templeton?   This is Charlie Walters. I have proposition for you."

24

Six weeks later, Leona stood at the front of the church alongside Betty who was dressed in an off-white dress with a lovely matching hat. Leona could only remember her looking so radiant one other time, when she married Vince. Betty's smile and the lilt in her walk left little doubt that she was doing the right thing for her.

Clarence was wearing his best suit and a million-dollar smile as he took Betty for his golden-age bride. Their children were there, not smiling, but with pleasant, unopposing looks on their faces. They didn't really approve of their father and their mother marrying at their advanced ages, but the pre-nup Clarence and Betty signed assuaged their feelings.

Leona glanced at the front row of church pews behind her. Her three foster boys were enrapt with the grand ceremony, having never seen such a spectacle. Doran couldn't quit playing with his tie, but at the moment, he seemed more interested in what the preacher said than his tie. She'd told Jaden that after the ceremony, there would be a feast with a very large cake so she suspected he was waiting intently for the end. Tiger seemed very pleased to be among this fine crowd and was on his best behavior.

As Clarence kissed his bride, everyone clapped until Jaden released a loud, "Let's eat!" The merriment over that declaration spread through the crowd as Betty and Clarence went back up the aisle. Leona signaled the boys to pull in behind her and off they went.

"Leona, you look lovely!" May hugged her warmly. "It was such a lovely ceremony. Simple and sweet. Didn't you think so, Carly?"

Carly smiled like someone backed in a corner who didn't want to fight. "Yes, lovely." She took a bite of her cake and swirled the crumbs around on her plate. "So Leona, those boys with you. How long are you going to keep them?" She looked out from under her fake eyelashes with self-righteousness.

Leona felt her anger rise to the tip of her tongue, but she bit it and kept the words from leaping out. "They are my foster sons. For now. I'll keep them until a better situation comes along or one of their relatives can take them. In the meantime, I'm tutoring them to get them caught up to grade level so we are pretty busy."

"They seem like nice kids," Nick said. "Amazing that they came out of the circumstances they did to be so well mannered."

"We've been working on that. Amazing how the promise of food can alter behavior in those who've done without it so often." Leona grew thoughtful. "They just want to be normal kids and have the things other kids do. They watched enough TV to know that living like they did wasn't normal and it wasn't the way they wanted to live. I'm happy to give them a taste of a good home. It's very fulfilling."

"And very Christian of you," Carly snorted.

"Give it a rest, Carly!" Irene said turning her back on the hateful woman. "You should show a little more charity yourself."

Carly harrumpfed and went away, taking Nick with her, but not before he threw an apologetic look toward Leona.

Irene and May stood with Leona. "I wonder why she's in our church group? She's not very charitable and certainly not the giving type."

May said, "I think Nick wants the group to be a good influence on her. But we can't make a silk purse out of a sow's ear."

"Oh, May!" Leona said laughing. "I can't believe you said that!" She took a sip of punch. "We're no tailors, are we." Chuckling they joined the rest of the party.

Later that night, the boys were almost too excited to go to bed. Leona tried to calm them by reading books to them. She sat on the edge of the bed, but had to leave the big ceiling light on to read.

"This would never do," Leona said, looking up at the ceiling light. "You needed a lamp and a nightstand for bedtime reading, Doran. That way you won't have to get out of bed to turn out the light. We'll look for one for you tomorrow."

Tiger looked puzzled. "What's a nightstand?"

"You know, it's that small piece of furniture beside my bed. Haven't you looked in my room?"

"You mean that little dresser with the lamp on it?"

Leona laughed. "Yes, that small dresser with the lamp and the alarm clock."

Tiger's eyebrows knitted together. "You got two of them. Do you need both of them?"

Leona stopped. The answer was so obvious. "You're right. I only need one. Let's go get that extra one for you to use."

The boys sprang out of bed and ran into her room with her close behind. She unplugged Joe's lamp and alarm clock and set them on the floor. The boys pulled the heavy nightstand away from the wall. As they did so, they heard a light clink. They tilted the stand to one side while Tiger looked under it. He came back up holding a gold ring in his hand. Joe's ring!

Leona gasped and grabbed it from the boy. She cradled it and a sob burst from her lips. The boys looked scared as the tears flowed down her face. "I found it! I found it! It must have fallen under there during the robbery and was hidden from the thieves." She clasped it in her hands and held it against her heart. With closed eyes, she offered up a silent prayer of thanks.

Opening her eyes again, she saw the frightened faces of the boys staring at her. She wiped her tears away and told them, "I'm crying because I'm so happy. This is the ring I was looking for when—when I found you." She gathered them all in a hug before helping them move the nightstand to their room.

The boys took the drawers out and hauled them to their room. Between Doran and Jaden, they wrestled the nightstand down the hall to their room and alongside their bed. Tiger brought the alarm clock and Leona carried in the lamp. She plugged everything in and set the right time on the clock.

"There. Now you can set the alarm and get yourselves up for school." She helped them into the large bed.

"Did you have a wedding like Miz Betty's?" Jaden asked as she tucked the boys in.

Leona smiled to herself. "Yes, a long time ago. I'll show you the pictures tomorrow if you'd like."

"What happened to your husband?"

"He had a bad disease and died. It was two and a half years ago." Her voice faded away as the memory threatened to take her out of the present.

"Do you think he'd have liked us? Would have let us stay here with you?"

Leona stared at three pairs of questioning eyes. If he'd been here, she'd never gone looking for her ring. She'd never have met these boys or seen how good hearts exist in terrible conditions. She'd have never known the joy of helping these boys with a chance to improve their lot in life.

"Granny Leona? You okay?" Doran took his arm out from under the covers and patted her hand.

She shook herself out of her runaway thoughts. "I'm not sure I'd ever have met you if he were here. I wouldn't have gone looking for my ring. T-bone would still be robbing houses and Smythe covering up for him. You'd still be with your mother..."

Jaden looked very sober. "Good thing your house got robbed then."

Tiger kicked his feet and Leona had to tuck him in again. "Yeah, I'm glad you got robbed too. I like it here!"

"Remember, you're only here until Miz Molly's new house is ready. Then you'll live with her so you can see your mom and uncle from time to time. But don't worry, you can come see me any time. Just call so I can give you a ride over. No more walking!" She tickled the boys and their laughter rang through the house. "Now get some sleep. You've had a big day."

Doran, the thoughtful thinker, piped in, "Should we tell the policeman thank you for having T-bone rob your house?"

Leona thought. That's what did it, the house robbery. It had changed her life in more ways than she thought possible. And it had changed Smythe's life too. And not for the better.

25

When Smythe opened the door of his modest home, Leona was shocked at his appearance. He looked like he'd aged a hundred years. His hair was uncombed and his face unshaven, and he was dressed in holey sweats. The faint smell of alcohol drifted out. He avoided prolonged eye contact with her, but she hoped by the time she left, he would.

"What do you want? To gloat? To check and make sure I'm wearing my ankle monitor?" He pulled up his pants leg to reveal the contraption around his lower leg. "See, it's there."

"I'm not checking up on you." Feeling embarrassed that he'd shown her his leg, she fumbled with her purse handle until her nerves got a little steadier. "I came to ask your forgiveness. I was very unpleasant to you and I'm sorry."

Smythe looked at her with raised eyebrows and a chuckle of disbelief. "You want my forgiveness? I don't believe you. Tell me why you're really here." He leaned on the door frame holding the door tight against him.

Leona didn't want to go home without finishing her mission. Betty had quoted Bible verses to her about forgiveness and with much prayer and thought, Leona decided she was right. To put this behind her, she had to set things right with Smythe. She cleared her throat. "Truly, I'm here to apologize for treating you badly."

"I don't have time for this." He moved to close the door.

Leona threw herself against the door to stop him from shutting it. In her haste, she knocked the door against him and he stumbled backward.

"Are you nuts? I should call the police! You're harassing and threatening me!"

Leona reached up and straightened her blouse that was askew. "No, please don't. I'm here," shouting louder than she realized, "to say I'm sorry. I don't want to go to hell for—"she hesitated and took a step back "—for being disrespectful to a police officer." It was her turn to look down at her feet and avoid eye contact.

Symthe let out a deafening roar disguised as a laugh. "So this is about your eternal soul? If you go to hell for being disrespectful, then there's no hope for me." He let go of the door and stood up straight. Sweeping his hand across his body and with a slight bow, he said, "I forgive you. You are absolved of your sins." He mockingly waved his hands in the shape of a cross.

Leona frowned. "Don't be sacrilegious about it. My apology is sincere. And I'm sorry about your wife, so I offer you my belated condolences as well. I lost my Joe to cancer and my heart still hurts with that loss. You probably feel the same way."

Her words must have struck a nerve. His stance softened and Leona thought she saw his eyes moisten.

"My wife. I'm glad she's not here to see me. She would be upset—ashamed of everything."

"If she'd had been here, none of this would have happened. Or I expect it wouldn't have."

Smythe sniffed. His jaw was working the muscles in the cheeks. "No, it wouldn't have. I didn't know what to do.

Her medicine was so expensive. Over $20,000 a month. I couldn't pay for it on a detective's salary. But I couldn't let her die because I didn't have the money. In the end, it didn't matter anyway. She died with the medicine. And I was in too deep in debt and too involved with T-bone to crawl out. He threatened to turn me in. To expose me as a crook. I panicked and—"

He sniffed again. Leona opened her purse and pulled out a little packet of tissues. He took one when she offered it and blew his nose.

"I should thank you for speaking for me at my hearing. The judge took into consideration how I was moving the boys to protect them from T-bone. She wouldn't have believed me if it hadn't been for you saying it. I don't know why you did that, but thank you."

"I did it because I found out the whole story. Miz Molly explained things to me. The boys told me that you'd told them you were getting them out of T-bone's reach. I hope that's true."

Smythe nodded his head as he ran his fingers through his graying hair. "T-bone's a bad dude and I knew if he thought the boys could finger him, he'd kill them. I couldn't let that happen. In spite of what you think of me, I was a good cop, before my wife got sick. I lost control trying to save my wife."

"That's understandable. And I'm the one who got them involved with T-bone." Leona let out a long sigh. "There's more than enough blame to go around. What concerns me now is that the boys are safe and in a good place."

"You're a good Christian woman, Leona."

"Thank you. I don't think you're a bad person. Just a person caught up in bad circumstances. Jesus said to pray for our enemies and I didn't do that. I'm sorry for that too. Maybe things would have turned out very differently if I had. Besides, I need to thank you for other things. I'm the boys' foster grandparent. Did you know?"

"No, I didn't."

Leona couldn't stop the smile from spreading across her face. "Yes, they are with me and I'm loving it. They're sweet kids. I keep in touch with Miz Molly and we visit every few weeks. They mean a lot to me and if it hadn't been for that burglary, I wouldn't have a purpose in my life again. So for whatever role you played in that, thank you."

Smythe shuffled his feet and stared at her. "You're unreal. Not many people like you around."

"Sounds crazy, huh. Life throws funny things at us and this time I got thrown over a cliff into a bed of roses. A few thorns here and there, but I mostly came out smelling sweet." She stared at him squarely. His eyes didn't hold hostility and his stance was relaxed. "We were once enemies. You think we can change that?"

Emotions faintly contorted Smythe's face. "In a way, you saved me. I got mixed up in that gang and I couldn't see a way out. Then you kept poking your nose into things that were putting you in danger. T-bone was out to get you because you were exposing our burglary ring. He wanted to kill you, but I kept telling him to leave you to me. I even planted drugs in your minivan, but then they weren't there. Whatever happened to those? Did you find them?"

"They were sucked out by a vacuum by accident." Shrugging, she gave him a crooked grin.

He tilted his head in a quizzical look, then shook it off. "T-bone tried to kill you with the drive-by shooting and when that didn't work, he decided to go after the boys. I couldn't let that happen."

"And I stopped you."

A soft chuckle escaped him. "You are tenacious. But I'm grateful. It forced me to do what I knew I should do. I'm the key witness against T-bone and his gang. They'll get put away for a long, long time."

"And your career is over. What will you do now?"

Smythe shrugged and shook his head. "I'll have to learn

a new trade while I'm on probation. I have to support myself somehow."

Leona gave him a reassuring smile. "Good luck in that endeavor. I'm sure you'll do fine once you find that new path." She watched his face flush as he looked away from her. "I'd like for you to consider coming to church with us."

He looked at his feet, silent for a long moment. "I'll think about it." He looked at her. "Want to come in? I just put a pot of coffee on."

"I'd love to. We have a lot to talk about."

He stood back and opened the door wide. "You don't happen to have any of Betty's cookies with you, do you?"

Leona let out a laugh and followed him inside.

.

ABOUT THE AUTHOR

C.S. Kjar lives with her long-time first husband in their empty nest. Since retiring, she and her husband travel quite a bit which gives her time to dream and imagine new stories and worlds. Her novels generally fall somewhere between the women's fiction and Christian fiction genres. She also writes an occasional children's book. When not writing or daydreaming, she loves to quilt, sew, and read to her grandsons.

Other Books by this Author:

The Treasure of Adonis

Five Grannies Go to the Ball

For more information on the author:

Visit my website at http://www.cskjar.com and my Facebook page at http://www.facebook.com/cskjar. You can also follow me on Twitter at @cskjar.

If you enjoyed this book, I would like to know about it. I would also appreciate it if you'd help others to enjoy this book too. How? Here's two ways to do that:

Recommend it: Tell your friends, readers' groups, and discussion boards about this book.

Review it: Tell other readers why you liked this book by reviewing it on Amazon or Goodreads. If you write a review, please send me an email at cskjar.books@gmail.com so I can thank you with a personal reply.

ACKNOWLEDGEMENTS

First and foremost, thanks to my husband who has put up with me all these decades and supports me in my writing career. Thanks to my children who have always encouraged me to follow my dreams.

Thanks to all of the people who put on the West Texas Writers Academy. Thanks for the instruction, opportunities, and networking that helped me hone my writing skills. The Academy put me on the right path to fulfill my goal of writing a book.

Thanks to Alexandra Sokoloff for teaching me how to plot a novel in a week. I walked into her class with plot two sentences long. By the end of the week, this book was plotted and ready to be written. Thanks to my classmates whose input helped this story come together. I'm not sure I could have completed this without you.

Made in the USA
San Bernardino, CA
15 July 2016